The Two-Faced Killer

Harborside Secrets – Book 3

Katy Pierce

Copyright © 2022 by Katy Pierce

All rights reserved.

No portion of this book may be reproduced in any form without written permission from the publisher or author, except as permitted by U.S. copyright law.

Contents

Description		V
Dedication		VII
1.	Chapter One	1
2.	Chapter Two	8
3.	Chapter Three	20
4.	Chapter Four	25
5.	Chapter Five	30
6.	Chapter Six	43
7.	Chapter Seven	47
8.	Chapter Eight	55
9.	Chapter Nine	59
10.	Chapter Ten	66
11.	Chapter Eleven	75
12.	Chapter Twelve	83
13.	Chapter Thirteen	87
14.	Chapter Fourteen	98

15.	Chapter Fifteen	109
16.	Chapter Sixteen	112
17.	Chapter Seventeen	121
18.	Chapter Eighteen	134
19.	Chapter Nineteen	139
20.	Chapter Twenty	146
21.	Chapter Twenty-One	155
22.	Chapter Twenty-Two	166
23.	Chapter Twenty-Three	174
24.	Chapter Twenty-Four	184
25.	Chapter Twenty-Five	191
26.	Chapter Twenty-Six	200
27.	Chapter Twenty-Seven	204
28.	Chapter Twenty-Eight	210
29.	Chapter Twenty-Nine	217
30.	Chapter Thirty	222
What's Next		229
A Note From The Author		232
Acknowledgments		234
About the Author		235

Description

For private investigator Carlee Knight, staying alive is a deadly tightrope walk. She truly believes her quest for justice will lead to her beloved twin brother's elusive killer—unless the killer catches her first.

Carlee's dramatic homecoming to her once-sleepy hometown makes the harsh reality that much clearer. It's not merely memories haunting Harborside anymore. For the first time since a mysterious serial killer butchered her eighth-grade class over a decade ago, a shadowy threat is hounding the town. Hounding Carlee, specifically, stalking her every move and creeping closer every night.

Its message is clear: back off or die.

As she races to identify her stalker before they strike again, Carlee's attention is pulled to a string of grisly murders in inner-city Chicago. Students of an elite beauty school are being found in deserted alleys, dressed in hideous clothes and posed for glamor shots—each with her throat slit.

The seedy trail of smeared lipstick and pooling blood drags Carlee into a dazzling subculture of runway divas, drugs, and posh queen-pins. A world in which every action is a statement and every look conceals a hidden truth.

Every second brings Carlee closer to answering her greatest fear: is the Eighth-Grade Killer really coming for her, or is this all the work of a copycat?

The Two-Faced Killer is the third book of Katy Pierce's unputdownable psychological thriller series, Harborside Secrets, where every choice carries secret consequences, and no character is safe from the villain's knife.

I'd like to dedicate this book to anyone who's afraid to walk away. If you're in a bad place, just get up and walk away. There's no need for you to explain yourself.

It's your life and it's the only one you'll ever get. Do what makes you happy.

Chapter One

Miranda's heels clicked against the sidewalk, her sore muscles working themselves out in the warmth of summer. She rolled her shoulders, counting the knots, each a physical reminder of stress and frustration. She loved balmy downtown Chicago nights like these, so what was it that was driving her nuts?

Oh, right.

"Can you believe that shit? A smokey eye... for a wedding?" Miranda asked, feeling a pang in her stiff neck as she glanced at the girl walking beside her. "I think she's going senile."

Giselle wasn't Miranda's best friend—not yet—but she was hands down her most tolerable classmate in the Advanced Bridal Makeup Workshop course. Maybe in the entire beauty school.

"I know, right?" Crossing her arms, Giselle blew out a long breath and laughed. It was a bitter sound, out of place in the pleasant evening. "It's like nobody at Aphrodite realizes how much we pay for these classes."

"Or gives a damn, more like," Miranda replied.

Dressed down for class, Miranda knew she and Giselle looked like what they were: a pair of stressed-out beauty students, not models, heading home after school to pout and complain. At least their makeup was impeccable—mostly, anyway. Hours of class under those harsh lights would put even the best foundation to the test.

Her eyeliner wings still needed a little help, but Miranda was confident she could make a name for herself the second she blew out of the Aphrodite Beauty Institute's front doors with her completed certifications. Then she needed bigger, better doors to open for her, which this program was *supposed* to arrange.

"I can't stand it," Miranda groaned. "I paid five hundred dollars for that 'cutting-edge, avant-garde' eye shadow. And did you see the look on that old bat's face? She thought she was blowing our minds."

"You bet I did. It's like she forgot we weren't the old retirement-home crones she teaches on the side."

"But that's just a rumor, right? I mean..." Miranda's immaculately sculpted brows arched behind her bangs. "She doesn't *really* do that, does she?"

Giselle snickered, rolling her eyes. "Oh, trust me, that's not a rumor. I saw a nursing home ID badge in her purse when I walked in."

"I swear, I'm going to lose my mind." Miranda rubbed at her temples. "I mean, I'm not a bad person, but half of these teachers are simply *ancient*, right? I'm not imagining that? I'm not just being a total asshole?"

"You're not. It's just the cold, hard truth of the industry, babe," Giselle said, shaking her head as she looked up at the night sky. "Some of them used to be hot shit, I'm sure, but now they're trying to teach us stuff we learned on the internet when we were eight. Hell, they just recently booted the dusty hag who used to teach the Runway Look class."

"Well, the clown they replaced her with isn't much better." Miranda gripped her sock bun at the base and pulled it looser, trying to ease her encroaching headache, exasperation oozing out of her. "Why are we paying for these classes if they're going to get geriatrics to teach us?"

"Girl, you aren't telling me anything I haven't already yelled at our faculty adviser," Giselle said, glowering at her water bottle as she unscrewed the cap. "Sometimes I wonder if the recruiter straight-up lied to us."

Miranda barely heard her, engrossed in her own thoughts. The staccato clacks of her heels built to a crescendo, the injustices of the beauty school manifesting in front of her.

"I don't know about you, but I signed up for this program because I was told I'd learn techniques that would take me to the next level," Miranda went on. "Shit, I needed this school to get me to New York or Paris or something! Something better than *Fashion Week–Wheaton*."

Giselle, mid-drink, spat around her water bottle and had to steady herself on Miranda's arm while she waffled between coughing and laughing. Feeling some of the tension ease, Miranda laughed too, and they continued down the sidewalk, arm in arm.

As their giggles subsided, Miranda considered Giselle's point: *the cold, hard truth of the industry*. It disturbed her a little, if she was being honest—how quickly a master makeup artist could wash up and wash out. After all, the "dusty hag" Giselle mentioned had once been an industry leader and worked with some of the biggest names in the business. Now she'd been pink-slipped by her own colleagues, no longer creative or innovative enough to train the next crop of beauty students. It was sad, watching someone so big fall so far.

Or it *would've* been sad, had Miranda not taken out a fat fucking loan to become one of said students.

At least it was only a few blocks from the school to Giselle's apartment, then a few more blocks in the opposite direction to her own place. As much as Miranda loved the warm breeze and the city lights, after four hours of class, she wanted nothing more than to fall onto her couch and watch TV until she passed out.

As they approached her walk-up, Giselle gave Miranda the customary goodnight hug she had given her each evening after class since they'd both started in the program last year.

"You know, if you moved into the apartment down the hall, you wouldn't have to walk down that creepy-ass alley anymore," Giselle said, a small but real worry in her eye. "My cousins could help you move your furniture."

Miranda chuckled, touched by her offer. "If you knew how much I was paying for my place, you'd be bugging me to help *you* move into *my* building. And as for any crackheads in that alley, that's why I've got this." She pulled a can of pepper spray out of her purse and shook it.

It wasn't some rinky-dink keychain pepper spray, either, but the kind that came in a canvas holster and was strong enough to put down a grizzly bear. She'd heard one too many horror stories about men who needed help understanding "no" and "go away."

"And besides," Miranda continued, "it's just one block, and it takes half the time."

"All right, but be sure—"

"To text you when I get to my place," Miranda finished, a genuine smile spreading across her cheeks. "I will, mother dearest."

Giselle rolled her eyes and slapped Miranda's shoulder, then slipped into her apartment, gently closing the door.

Miranda turned on her heel, doubling back to the main street and toward Aphrodite. It wasn't long before she turned down the dark alley behind the school's storage building—a straight shot to her apartment.

She had taken this path countless times before, at least twice a week, after every class with Giselle. She knew its strange sounds like the back of her hand—the odd street cat rooting around in a trash bag, the soft hum of a car pulling out of the underground garage. Nothing had ever really spooked her.

But that night felt different.

Try as she might, she couldn't figure out exactly *why* it felt different. The hairs on her forearms stood on end, and her breathing grew shallow. Her eyes darted from one lump of trash to another, looking for something—anything—out of place.

"I must be losing my damned mind," Miranda murmured, doing her best to shake off the feeling. Her footsteps quickened across the asphalt.

Each clip-clop of her shoes echoed off the steel shutters and dumpsters that lined the alley. The once-pleasant heat took on a claustrophobic quality, like it was reaching into her chest and trying to strangle her from the inside.

"The hell is wrong with you, girl?" she whispered. She prided herself on not being easily scared. Whenever her friends would watch a scary movie, she was the one who had to calm everyone else down.

If she were in a horror movie right now, the killer would be crouched in a shadowy nook down this very alley, waiting for her. Then, once she was close enough...

Crash!

A trash can just behind her clattered to the pavement, sending Miranda bolting like an Olympic sprinter. She made it fifteen feet—halfway down the alley—before something limp and solid caught her ankle. Her large bag dropped to the dirty asphalt and she staggered forward, her palms burning as she caught herself against the rough brick siding of the school. She could hear whoever had tipped over the can padding closer, creeping up behind her. Groping inside her purse, she grabbed the pepper spray.

Knees knocking, hands shaking, Miranda let out a growl as she pulled the canister free from its holster and whipped around, leveling it in the direction of her unseen pursuer. "Back off, asshole!" she shouted into the night.

An old mutt, gray whiskers and all, blinked back at her, entirely unthreatened. It cocked its head quizzically before a car passing the far end of the alley slammed on the horn, and the dog took off.

Despite herself, Miranda laughed. Relief flooded her veins, diluting the adrenaline, and with it came the realization that she'd let Giselle's worry infect her. She tucked the pepper spray back into her purse before clacking up the shadowy alley, looking for her dropped bag.

She found it—barely. Snatching up the strap, she dropped it just as quickly when her hand met damp faux-leather.

"Damn it!" Apparently, it had fallen into a puddle. She shivered, hoping it was water and not urine. "Barely two weeks old too…"

She brushed at the spot on her bag—felt the slickness, the oily quality, and knew it wasn't water. Or urine.

A foul curiosity compelled her to sniff her palm, and she gagged at the metallic stench. Miranda dug out her cell phone, using the light to see where the bag had landed, to follow the trail of mysterious fluid up to…

"A shoe? What the hell?" she muttered, reaching down to pick up the tacky vinyl heel sticking out from a pile of cardboard boxes, likely a bunch of studio waste some lazy custodian had pushed up against the wall. She tugged at the shoe. Its resistance momentarily baffled her before she realized—it was still connected to a foot.

"Please let this be a mannequin," she breathed, her stare fixated on the ankle jutting out from beneath the stack of junk. "Please let this be the stupid school throwing away a perfectly good mannequin..."

Angling her cell phone flashlight, she discovered that the mound wasn't a pile of cardboard, but a single broken-down box laid gently over something, like a curtain at a theater. Her hands shook as she slowly pulled it away.

Miranda nearly had her second heart attack of the evening.

"It *is* a mannequin," she huffed, "but a horrific one."

A round face stared back at her, pale and glassy-eyed under a floppy sun hat. The mannequin's limbs were crossed daintily as if posed for a boudoir photoshoot, its thin body draped in a flowery yellow dress several sizes too large. Propped gently in the puddle of dark liquid, it stared back at her, a deranged lipstick smile plastered on its face, its cheeks slathered with garish, clown-like makeup.

"Hang on..." Stomach dropping, Miranda examined her wet palm in the light of her phone. *Red*.

She screamed.

It wasn't a mannequin.

Mannequins didn't bleed.

Chapter Two

Carlee Knight let out a curse as she ran face-first into the glass of her office suite door.

"What the hell is going on out there?" Eleanor's muffled voice asked from inside.

"Nothing!" she called back. Realization washed over her sleep-deprived brain. Carlee had been so tired lately, stirred from sleep by nightmare after nightmare, she'd tried to verbally order her office door open—as if her trusty AI assistant lived in her brain rather than in the walls of her condo.

"Everything's fine," she lied. The truth was, she hadn't even looked at the handle. She'd just said, "Archibald, hold the door, please," and waltzed right into it.

"Are you okay?" Eleanor asked, eyeing the imprint of her face on the glass.

Carlee held her beet-red nose as she manually cranked open the door. "It's too early for this shit."

"Actually, it's almost nine," Eleanor countered matter-of-factly, returning to the newspaper she was reading behind her desk.

"Like I said. Too early." Carlee gave her nose one last rub and tried her best to shake off the fatigue of her daily run. "Good morning, by the way."

"As it happens, I figured you'd be a little out of sorts." Eleanor nodded to a cup of coffee on her desk, steam still wafting from the top.

"Oh, you are a goddess." Carlee grabbed it greedily and took a sip, not caring if she burned her tongue. Maybe it was the placebo effect, but she could already feel the caffeine making its way into her system. "Anything new in there for me?" she added, nodding toward the paper in Eleanor's hand.

"Not that I've seen, no. At least, nothing helpful for your current case." Eleanor's mature and elegant face, combined with her stylish business-casual outfit, gave her the air of an executive disappointed in her most recent investment's short-term return rather than a PI's assistant researching a murder.

Carlee had been scouring the internet for new information on Janie Toland, the latest potential victim of the supposed Two-Faced Killer, who was said to have resurfaced after thirty years of inactivity. Three days ago, she'd read an article about reemerging serial killers—which mentioned Joel Barclay and the Eighth-Grade Killer as well—and since then, had been itching to stick her fingers into the Two-Faced Killer case.

The article posited that this recent spate of killings from long-dormant serial killers might be the work of a copycat. Carlee couldn't rest until she got to the bottom of it. She'd called every journalist with a byline about Janie Toland, but even the first reporter to break the story had nothing new for her, simply regurgitating press releases from the Chicago Police. The case was too new and too active for any accurate, helpful information to be released to the public eye.

"As I mentioned before..." Eleanor put the paper down with a sigh and targeted Carlee with a hard look. "I know you've set your mind on this, but I don't think getting involved is good for you."

"I know you don't. You've made that quite clear."

"And yet, here you are. Walking face-first into the office door," Eleanor said, her graceful features adopting stern lines. "This isn't healthy, Carlee. You're going to get in too deep and work yourself into some paranoid episode if you keep getting thrown into these murder cases and dangerous situations."

"So much for being a goddess." Bitterness rose in Carlee's mouth. She took another sip of coffee, more to give her hands something to do than anything else. "Give me a little credit."

"Believe me, I am. I know you, Carlee. And I know you're going to become a shell of your former self if you keep going down this path."

"So!" Carlee clanked the mug on the desk with enough force to make Eleanor jump in her seat. "Is that all?"

Eleanor shot her one last chary, sidelong look. "I guess it is."

"Then I'll be in my office," Carlee said, turning toward the door. She closed it behind her—not quite a slam but certainly not softly—and drew a deep breath. It was, beyond a shadow of a doubt, too early for any of this.

Tossing her bag on the floor, she moved around her desk, picking up Mocha as she fell into her chair. She popped his control panel open and ran a line to her personal digital assistant for diagnostics. As always, he was working optimally, but she needed to do something that would lower her blood pressure, and taking care of Mocha always calmed her.

He beeped brightly in her hands. It was just a signal that he had successfully paired with the PDA, but Carlee liked to think it was his way of saying "good morning." She smiled to herself.

"You're not going to give me any lectures, are you, Mocha?" she asked him quietly. "Nope, you have no thoughts about what's best for me. You're helpful and blissfully ignorant. Just the way I like you."

He beeped again and whirred his rotors. His systems were working as expected, so she rested him on her lap and dug her cell phone out of her pocket, pausing with her thumb lingering over the screen. She chewed on the inside of her cheek.

"It wouldn't be too soon to call Zack, would it?" she wondered aloud, raising her eyebrow at Mocha when he let out another soft beep.

Zack West was obviously a workaholic too. Even with the added pressure of his city detective duties, he'd thrown himself full-force into her previous case, if for no other reason than because Carlee asked for help. Still, the Toland case was in its early stages, and she worried that if she called now, it would only annoy him. She didn't need to get stonewalled right out of the gate, especially with how grumpy Zack could be when he thought Carlee was chasing a dead end.

But at the same time, these first few days were integral to catching the Two-Faced Killer—or whoever had murdered Janie Toland.

Carlee eyed the office door. She normally ran *should-I-or-shouldn't-I* problems by Eleanor, but given how many lectures she'd received lately, that wasn't an appealing option. For the past few days, Eleanor had been scolding her to stop investigating this case, insisting that it was for her own good.

But Carlee couldn't stop. She had to keep going, keep peeling back the layers, and solve this murder. If the Two-Faced Killer *was* a copycat, then Joel Barclay's killer could be a copycat as well, and *that* might mean she wasn't really in danger. Plus, catching a fake Eighth-Grade Killer could lead to catching the real one, and that was more than she'd ever had to go on before.

It was a stretch, but Carlee needed to know if the Eighth-Grade Killer was back, and in that endeavor, she would chase any possible lead. Justice for Cameron, for all the victims, hung in the balance.

She looked down at her phone. Maybe Ian Garnett, the prettiest face at the Chicago FBI, would be willing to help his off-the-books private investigator colleague untangle yet another mystery. He'd always been helpful before.

Maybe even too *helpful*, she thought, remembering how he'd butted into her last case entirely uninvited.

The PDA chirped, finishing its Mocha diagnostics. Carlee pulled the drone's remote from her top drawer and spun him up, leaving him hovering two feet off the desk. He tilted to-and-fro, all lights coming up green.

As she watched Mocha hover like a flying saucer, she weighed her options. She was hesitant to admit it, but she found herself leaning toward Zack for more than just professional reasons. He was an incredibly passionate investigator underneath the gruff and silent exterior, and he'd warmed to Carlee considerably in the past few weeks. Solving gruesome murders together and saving a man's brother-in-law tended to have that effect on people.

She exchanged Mocha's remote for her phone and dialed.

"Hey, Zack—it's Carlee," she blurted the instant he picked up, before he could even say hello.

"I can read a caller ID," he answered, as if phone calls were a chore to him.

Worry zipped through her. Had she already blown her chance at securing Zack as her partner on the Toland case? As her friend? "Okay, and I can read the room, so I'll save you some time and cut to the chase. I was hoping you could help me on a case I'm looking into."

"The Two-Faced Killer case," Zack said flatly, making Carlee's skin crawl.

"How'd you know?"

"Call it a gut feeling." His gut feelings had sparked several serious fights between them so far, but this time, Carlee detected a hint of a smile in his voice. "I've been waiting for your call since that article got published. So, what do you need?"

"I was just wondering if you could maybe, possibly, slip the police records my way."

"Do you have a lead?"

"All I have is a theory, and I want to test it, but I can't do that without knowing exactly what we're looking at."

"A theory, huh?" He snorted. She could hear papers shuffling on his desk, and something in the way he spoke deflated her buoyant hope. "Well, Carlee, I'd love to help you out on that," Zack said, and she knew the "but" was coming. "But it *might* cause a few problems on my end."

"Such as...?" she pushed, sliding back in her chair.

"Such as the fact that I'm not even assigned to the case. Such as the fact that this case isn't even in my precinct. Such as the fact that—" She could imagine him counting off the list on his fingers, so she stopped him midway.

"But it could be related to the Eighth-Grade Killer!" Carlee winced, realizing she was precariously close to begging. She was *not* going to beg for help from a cop, even a cop who had not so long ago peeled her butt off the pavement after a witness took umbrage to her questions.

"I don't know, Carlee..." His pause lingered so long, she thought she'd lost the connection. "I considered it, but I'm not sure these cases are connected."

"Think again, Zack," Carlee not-begged, hoping her arguments might convince him when they hadn't even convinced her. "Two dormant serial killers, long since thought 'retired,' reappear within a month of each other? Within miles of each other? What are the chances?"

Another grim, unfriendly pause.

"Pretty slim," Zack admitted. "But that's hardly evidence, and you're the one who always barks about following the trail of concrete—"

"Exactly—pretty slim," she repeated, blowing past the rest of it. "So what if it's *not* the real Two-Faced Killer? *Not* the real Eighth-Grade Killer? What if it really is a copycat?"

Zack snorted again. "Don't tell me you're actually drinking that reporter's Kool-Aid. You know that sounds completely paranoid, right?"

"And you sound like my very argumentative secretary."

"Then your secretary knows what she's talking about. It's a shot in the dark, Carlee. At the very best."

"I know. But it *is* a possibility," she said a little desperately. He hadn't said no, and she'd keep trying until he did. "All we need is a reason to investigate the case. It doesn't have to be the right reason."

Silence again. Then, hesitantly, "It's paper-thin, Carlee. Thinner, maybe."

"Crappy-pancake thin? Cheap-stockings thin? Zack West's-patience thin?" she needled, enjoying the mental image of his shoulders rising with each jab. "Give me some specifics, Detective."

Carlee heard him tapping on his desk, the physical manifestation of gears turning in his head. She knew from experience that the best way to handle someone like Zack was to get him simmering, then sit and wait for him to come to her. So she waited, pulling over Mocha's remote to fly him around while cradling the phone between her shoulder and ear.

"You know what?" he barked, finally.

"What?"

"Fuck it." He huffed into the receiver, and she knew she had him. "We've got zero leads on the Eighth-Grade Killer right now."

"So... does that mean you're in?"

"Sure, what the hell. Might as well pursue whatever avenues open up."

"I really do think something's going on here," she stressed before he could change his mind. She shot up from her chair, and Mocha shot up with her, nearly flying into the ceiling. She quickly landed him back on her desk. "These copycat murders—if they are copycat murders—have happened too close together to be a coincidence."

"It could very well be a coincidence," Zack said. "We know next to nothing about Janie Toland's case yet, and ninety-nine percent of the things we *do* know don't point to the Eighth-Grade Killer."

"Call it a gut feeling."

"You don't have those, remember?" Zack gruffed. "Anyway, I can tell you're invested in this, and you were right last time, so I'll throw you a bone and pull some files for you."

She let a smile curl her mouth until her muscles stung. "Thanks, Zack. I mean it."

"Wow... gratitude. That's a new look on you."

"It's not gratitude. It's relief."

"Relief?" She heard a faint creak over the line, like Zack had leaned forward in his chair.

"That you're willing to help. It would've been really awkward for both of us if you'd refused and I had to hack into your computer and download whatever I needed."

"You're... kidding, right?" he asked half-jokingly. "Can you seriously do that?"

She shrugged even though he couldn't see her. "I prefer not to answer that question on the grounds that it would incriminate me."

"You're kidding. I've decided, for my sanity, that you're kidding."

Carlee kept mum.

"In any case, the way I see it, the only reason my brother-in-law is alive—hell, the only reason *I'm* alive—is because of you. The least I can do is annoy some other detectives and grease the wheels for you."

"How fast do you think you can get it done?"

"Annoy my fellow detectives? You'd be surprised," Zack said. "I'll get some docs and meet you at the coffee shop tomorrow."

"You can call it the Catty Corner, you know. That is its name."

"I'm not calling it that." She could almost see Zack's grimace. "Why couldn't they just go with a coffee pun like everybody else?"

Carlee laughed, hung up, and began a mental inventory of tech that might be helpful to the investigation. She would bring Mocha along on any intelligence-gathering missions, of course, but she had a couple of prototypes that might prove their usefulness as well. She was nearly through her checklist when Eleanor's knuckles peppered the door—the faint but firm tap that signaled she wasn't willing to apologize but was no longer actively angry with Carlee.

"Come in," Carlee called, and Eleanor poked her head in.

"There's a Sharon Campbell on line one waiting for you. Would you like me to put her through or take a message?"

The name stopped Carlee dead in her tracks, evaporating all thoughts of the Toland case or drones or checklists. Eleanor must've glimpsed the shock on her face because she cocked her head and raised an eyebrow.

"You know this woman?" she asked, a protective edge to her voice.

"I... used to."

"Is she bad news?"

"No! No, it's not that at all," Carlee half shouted, coming out of her near-catatonic state. "It's just that I haven't heard the name in a while. She's—she was—the mother of my best friend. Back in, um, middle school." Her gaze dropped to the floor as she forced the words out. "In eighth grade."

Sharon Campbell, mother of Addison Campbell—cute, funny, popular, sweet Addison. She had been one of the only children in Harborside to befriend the shy and geeky Carlee Knight, breaking through her shell and practically dragging her out of her comfort zone. Even back then, Carlee knew Addison was destined for great things.

Until the Eighth-Grade Killer had taken everything from her.

Guilt enveloped Carlee. Sharon had never been anything but loving and kind to her, but talking with the poor woman brought up terrible memories that all but left Carlee wishing she had been killed instead of Addison.

"Why would she call now?" she asked Eleanor.

"Maybe she saw that article."

"I... guess so," Carlee stammered. If Sharon was trying to get ahold of her, it couldn't be for anything good. "Just tell her I'm busy."

Eleanor nodded slowly. "Sure thing."

"No, wait! Could you tell her I'm out on a case and can't take any calls or clients?"

"I can do that too." Eleanor nodded again, understandingly, and—thank god for her—didn't ask why.

"Thanks!" Carlee blurted as Eleanor returned to her desk, letting the office door softly click shut behind her.

Carlee went into overdrive, stuffing drones into their cases and packing them into a bag. Finally, she slunk to the door and cracked it open, feeling like a child peeking out to see if the school principal was still cross with her. She waited for Eleanor to hang up with Sharon before slipping out.

"What did she say?"

"Nothing. She didn't want to leave a message, I'm afraid. She just said she's going to try back in a few days," Eleanor explained, offering Carlee an apologetic look.

"That's fine." Carlee waved her off, even though it wasn't fine—not at all. Her stomach churned. "I'm heading out to go over some records."

"Wait, I want to know why this—"

"Bye, Eleanor! We'll talk later!" she chirped with performative cheerfulness, and then she was out the door and heading down to the street where her car was parked. Fighting with her grumbling gut, she almost felt normal by the time she opened the front door.

Until she saw the brown box perched on the hood of her car.

Fight-or-flight instincts kicking in, Carlee frantically checked up and down the street for potential threats. There was nothing but an onrush of cars, the sounds of downtown traffic buzzing in her ears. She snatched the box and ducked back inside, cramming her body into the business stairwell, heart hammering, neck sweating.

Part of her wanted—demanded—to chuck the package into the nearest dumpster, but she knew she couldn't. Whatever was in this box might help her identify her stalker, and besides, she had to look at the threat head-on or she'd never stop thinking about it. It was the way the world and her past had made Carlee Knight.

The box was painfully cold in her hands, or was it her fingers that were so icy? She shook as she peeled back the top flap. A whoosh of vapor hit her in the face as the dry ice inside could finally breathe again.

But there was something else.

"Is that...?" She peered inside, squinting as the fog slowly dispersed.

"What the shit!" she yelled, letting the box fall to the ground.

It rolled right out onto the linoleum of her office building.

A crimson spill along with a human-sized heart.

Chapter Three

Carlee had never seen someone struggle not to choke on his coffee quite as theatrically as Zack West. He ended up with a hacking cough that drew the eyes of every patron in the Catty Corner Café, and Carlee wouldn't have been surprised if his big raspy woofs startled a passerby or two on the sidewalk outside.

"A *heart*," Zack managed between coughs.

"That's what I said."

"As in, an actual heart?"

"It was a heart."

"But a real one? Not a fake one? Not rubber? But an actual heart. In a box. On your car."

She nodded. It wasn't a comforting reaction from a detective, but she supposed there was no way to console someone about an unscheduled organ delivery.

"Eleanor called the cops right away," she explained, stirring her coffee with the stick. "It didn't take long to find out it was a sheep heart—not human—but that didn't stop it from scaring the absolute shit out of me."

"You've got cameras all around that place, don't you?" Zack asked, a hint of concern creeping into his ordinarily stoic voice, his eyebrows knitting together. His light-gray suit matched his salt-and-pepper hair and helped him stand out as a serious man in a decidedly unserious coffee shop.

"I do, but there was nothing on them."

"*Nothing?*"

"Nothing. I managed to park right at the edge of my camera coverage. Whoever did it practically tossed the box onto my car. Didn't show up on a single frame."

"Damn. But someone must've seen something, right? It's downtown—business cameras everywhere. Cell phones, bystanders..."

"I'm asking around, but I'm not holding my breath." Carlee sighed. "You'd be surprised how many people opt for the absolute minimum in security. A crappy camera, one guard asleep at the front desk... or whatever will get the insurance agent off their backs."

She sucked her teeth and took a frustrated sip of coffee. Her relative calmness since yesterday disturbed Carlee as much as the messages themselves. The existential threat of these letters and packages was being dulled by their frequency, and somehow, as crazy as it seemed, she was ready to get back to work. Maybe Eleanor had a point about the path Carlee had chosen.

Still, sitting in a coffee shop with Zack and a dozen witnesses felt about as safe as she could be outside of her apartment, the impenetrable Castle Carlee.

"If you don't mind, do you think we could talk about the Toland case?" she asked, scrunching one eye quizzically. Zack shot her a concerned look over his steaming mug of black coffee.

"Excuse me for finding a heart delivery to be an irregular thing worth talking about."

"I'd just like to get my mind off sheep hearts and focus on doing something worthwhile."

He rubbed his chin, thinking her request over. "Well, if you're sure..."

"I'm sure," she promised, and he nodded, sighing as if he understood.

She'd been worried Zack would interrogate her to ascertain her mental state, something Ian certainly would've done, and his agreement to move forward was a breath of fresh air. He slipped the folders across the table, and Carlee cut her gulp of coffee short in her hurry to pick up the top folder.

"We're still waiting on Janie Toland's autopsy," he said, "but it should be done in the next day or so. I know the medical examiner personally, and she does good work."

Carlee opened the folder to find a photo of Janie, gaudily made-up, her throat slit nearly to the bone. The hallmarks of the Two-Faced Killer.

"No one we've interviewed seems to have any idea who would want to do something like this to Miss Toland," Zack continued. "Her friends and family agree she was well-liked in her social circles and at the beauty school she was attending."

"Not surprising," she said, flipping through photo after macabre photo, her mood growing six shades darker. "Serial killers don't typically have personal vendettas against their victims. Any signs of sexual assault?"

"None. And based on the bloodstains, she was dressed, posed, and made-up before she was killed."

"In keeping with the Two-Faced Killer's MO," Carlee added, glancing up just long enough to catch Zack's skeptical look.

The blood from Janie's wound fell down the front of her dress and pooled on the cardboard in the alleyway. Closer inspection showed no defensive injuries on her arms. Janie had not fought back or even grabbed at her throat as she bled out. A chill spiked up Carlee's spine, colder and sharper than the dry ice from yesterday.

"If this is a copycat," she finally said, reaching for the next folder in the stack, "they've done their homework, that's for sure. What do we know about Janie herself?"

"She was twenty-four years old, a student at the Aphrodite Beauty Institute. According to school records, she was talented and would've done well for herself after graduating. She wanted to get into modeling and professional makeup production."

"Is that a competitive industry?" A circus of murderous suburban realtors flashed through her recent memory—remnants of her last hard-won case. "Maybe someone wanted to get rid of the competition?"

"It's competitive, but we don't have any reason to think she was killed by a business rival," Zack said. "She hadn't even started her career. No connections, no internships... nothing beyond that school."

"Do we think this might've been personal? Jealousy?" she asked, leafing through the documents. "Maybe she overshadowed her classmates and someone got revenge by dressing her up like some showgirl off the Vegas Strip."

He shook his head. "I think that's a reach. All her classmates and teachers spoke highly of her."

Carlee pointed at the document. "It says here that she was taking night classes. What did she do during the day?"

"Worked full-time as a waitress at a small café near the institute. Moonlit doing amateur gigs, handled a few friends' bridal parties, stuff like that."

"The Two-Faced Killer originally targeted models and makeup artists," she said, flipping through printouts of Janie's recent social media posts, which were mostly pictures of her cosmetic work. "Still following the pattern. The question is, why come back after thirty years?"

"And why target Janie?" Zack added.

Bzzt!

Zack's phone buzzed on the table. He checked the text message casually enough, but the way his brow rumpled told Carlee that whatever it said was unexpected—and troubling.

"Ah, shit," he grouched, standing up from his chair.

"What happened?"

"It's the detective I got these files from. We need to go right now!" Zack was already stalking toward the door, leaving his coffee, the documents, and Carlee behind.

"Damn it, Zack!" Leaping up, she scrambled to stuff the pages back into their folders. "What is it? What the hell did they say?"

Zack paused with the café door half open, impatiently scowling over his shoulder like he hadn't left Carlee sitting there with highly sensitive material spread across the table. "Someone reported a woman walking around in a daze in Millennium Park!"

"So…?"

"So we need to get to Wrigley Square ASAP. According to the report, she's wearing tacky clothes and terrible makeup."

Carlee's eyes went wide. A second victim. *Still alive!*

Shoving the last of the case folders into her bag, she shot out of the booth to chase after him. Millennium Park was only a couple blocks away, and they could be there in minutes if they hurried.

If this was indeed a victim of the Two-Faced Killer, then every passing second meant they might already be too late.

Chapter Four

Carlee skidded to a stop next to Zack at the corner of Millennium Park, a siren blaring in the distance. They had been in the perfect spot to respond to the call and had managed to get to the scene before any uniforms—police, medical, or otherwise.

"Do you see anything?" she asked, dread pitching her voice low. Her head whipped around, searching for a strangely dressed woman amid the throngs of pedestrians, neat rows of trees, and tennis courts.

Just because they had beaten first responders didn't mean they had beaten everyone. If this was, in fact, a runaway victim of the Two-Faced Killer or a copycat, then a murderer could be circling the park, looking for their escaped prey. If Carlee and Zack didn't find this woman first, she might wind up in an alley with her throat slit.

"CPD fucked up thirty years ago, letting this sick bastard get away," Zack said, winded from their dash to the park as he stalked into a pack of tourists, stopping for no one. "Out of the way!" he barked, and the group parted like small fishes flitting away from a shark.

"Calm down." Carlee knew her words weren't going to help him calm down.

"I'll be damned if I let them kill someone else on my watch." He took off diagonally, deeper into the massive city park, Carlee sprinting to catch up.

As she closed the distance between them, a thought nagged at her. The time between this murderer's kills—or attempted kills—had been frighteningly short. Fewer than five days. The Eighth-Grade Killer had taken weeks, and sometimes months, between each attack.

They hadn't made it a hundred yards into the park, their feet scraping against the concrete path, before they found a crowd gathering, curious and fearful in turn. Carlee and Zack made their way over, almost getting hit by a pair of cyclists who were also distracted by the crowd.

In their midst, a woman—wearing a pink and orange cocktail dress that was too big for her—was limping slowly, absently, across the grass. It was an odd scene, completely out of place in the sunny park, a gentle breeze wafting between the tree leaves. A few nearby college kids murmured something unkind about "crazy homeless people" as the woman stumbled and fell toward one of them, who shoved her back.

"What the hell?" Carlee shouted, ducking and weaving her way through the crowd to plant herself firmly between the teenagers and the woman. "You kids better back up and back off before—"

"Everyone disperse—right now!" Zack ordered, holding his detective's shield up for all to see. "This is a Chicago Police matter!"

Between Zack's command and Carlee's glare, the crowd wandered off, and she caught the shuffling woman by the shoulders, steadying her. "Hey, shh... it's okay," she soothed. "We're here to help you. Can you understand me?"

A few onlookers lingered, watching to see what might happen next. Carlee didn't care as long as they didn't try to interfere.

"Ma'am, my name is Detective West," Zack said, approaching the woman as calmly and unthreateningly as possible. "Can you tell me what happened?"

The woman looked around, her glassy hazel eyes not focusing on anything in particular. Her lips quirked between a smile and a frown, and her pupils were blown as wide as a cat's.

"She's in some sort of a trance." Carlee reached for her arm, trying to stop her from drifting as the distant sirens grew louder. She gently tapped the woman's shoulder to get her attention, hoping a dose of friendliness might help her talk. "My name is Carlee. Carlee Knight."

It was a gambit to see if the woman's subconscious would grab ahold of an easy autopilot task—introducing herself—but to Carlee's dismay, it didn't work.

"Hey, can you hear me at all?" Carlee asked. "What's your name?"

Only unintelligible babble came out, and her head slumped back and forth on her weak neck.

"Jesus. Is she crying?" Carlee ran a thumb under the woman's eye, gently wiping away a tear. The woman didn't react.

Carlee pulled back her hand and found a thick white foundation coating her skin. Her thumb had left a streak in the caked-on makeup. It was clownish, degrading, childish. This was not merely the work of someone who didn't know their way around a vial of mascara—this makeup had been *deliberately* botched... and recently.

"Holy shit, Zack," Carlee breathed. "Are you seeing this?"

"It's kind of hard to miss."

Together, they helped the woman sit down on the grass. Zack squatted beside her, waving his hands in front of her face, mere inches from her eyes, and snapped twice. She didn't even blink.

The Two-Faced Killer targeted models and industry professionals, people at the pinnacle of fashion. The bad makeup and tacky clothes were calculated insults, meant to lay those people low. This woman carried all the signs of a Two-Faced victim—everything except the slit throat.

"How the hell did she get here?" Carlee muttered, dragging her palm through the grass to clean it of foundation. "And how did she get away?"

Zack's reply was interrupted by the arrival of medical personnel. As the ambulance pulled onto the sidewalk, accompanied by a police car, he stood up and waved his arm broadly, flagging them down. "Keep an eye on her," he said. "I'm going to go bring them in."

Zack took off at a jog, leaving Carlee alone with the woman and a handful of onlookers. Without the presence of a physically imposing police detective, some of the crowd began to close in again.

"For the last time, everybody back the fuck up!" Carlee shouted. To her, they were nothing but vultures circling a meal. She rested her arm protectively around the woman's shoulders, speaking with the soft, sympathetic cadence her mother had used whenever Carlee or her brother skinned their knees. "I don't know if you can understand me right now, but we're going to take care of you. The paramedics will take you to a doctor and clean you up. You're going to be fine."

"I..." The woman's mouth hung open as if she was trying to say more, and Carlee leaned forward, worried she might miss something.

This experience was the closest thing to a break the Two-Faced Killer case ever had. Carlee could save lives by helping the police better understand the killer's victim selection process, and she might even lead investigators to the murderer...

If this woman had seen her attacker's face.

If she even remembered anything once she woke up from the daze she was in.

If she survived.

"Don't worry about anything. Just..." Carlee stammered, struggling to find something to say, watching the woman's mouth close and her round eyes stare childishly at the sky. "Just stay calm and keep breathing. Promise me?"

The woman's head stopped bobbing for a moment—just a moment—and, with a twinkling of comprehension in her eyes, slowly turned to face Carlee. The cloudiness in her gaze seemed to disperse, and she finally found her voice.

"Why did... why... who..."

Carlee hung on every whispered word. But before she could finish, the moment of clarity slipped out of her mouth and floated away.

Within seconds, the cloudiness returned, and her head dropped suddenly on her neck, her eyes rolling back into her head.

"No—*live*, god damn it," Carlee spat, listening to the footfalls of the paramedics as they rushed toward her. "You have to live!"

Chapter Five

The buzz of the elevator's slow rise was drowned out by the Muzak—some odd, synthy eighties beat that was loosening Carlee's grip on her sanity with every second. She was only drawn back to the present with a loud snap of Zack's fingers in her face.

"Mission Control to Carlee Knight," he barked, probably mistaking her inattention for boredom. Shaking away her spiral of gloomy thoughts, she didn't have the heart to argue. Not this time.

"Sorry," she muttered. "I'm listening, I swear. What were you going to say about Janie's autopsy?"

"I said they found a boatload of ketamine in her system." Zack crossed his arms, watching the numbers over the door climb at a glacial pace. Now that the autopsy report had been completed, they were stuck in this unassuming apartment elevator on business, hoping to speak to one of Janie's closest friends.

"What else? I need specifics," Carlee snapped, rubbing her temples. She had a migraine brewing, and the music's awful beat was drilling into her forebrain. "How much, and how did it affect her?"

"Not enough to kill her—cause of death was, unsurprisingly, the slit throat."

"But at least now we have a definite explanation for the lack of defensive wounds and the pooling blood. Her throat must've been cut right there, in the alley."

"That's what it looks like," Zack said, his jaw set grimly. "She was basically a mannequin at the end."

Carlee bit her lip. She tried to put herself in Janie's shoes: caught in a drug-induced haze, unable to fight back, barely even aware the end was drawing near. Her fists clenched at her sides.

"I'm going to catch this fucker, Zack. If it's the last thing I do," she said. "Were they able to determine whether Janie injected the ketamine herself or if someone else did?"

"Does it matter?"

"Well... Maybe the killer is targeting drug users in the industry. If not, they'd need their own source. Could be worth looking into."

Zack shook his head. "The angle of the injection site wasn't clean. Could've been she was new to using or could've been the killer getting frustrated. We don't know. But we *do* know the Two-Faced Killer originally used Rohypnol, not ketamine."

Carlee sighed. "Chalk up another point for 'copycat.' But in and of itself, that fact isn't conclusive. It's possible the original Two-Faced Killer's methods have evolved."

Zack nodded. "Right. Maybe they have easier access to ketamine now. I'd bet dollars to donuts that the tox screen on the Jane Doe will light up with ketamine."

The woman they'd found in the park yesterday was currently unconscious at Chicago Memorial Hospital, still in critical condition. The initial report determined she was definitely drugged, but they still weren't clear on the substance involved. How she had managed to get away from her attacker without being otherwise harmed was still a mystery, presuming there *was* an attacker. Either way, she was fighting for her life with every hour.

The elevator finally dinged, and the door slid open.

Carlee mulled over the case facts as they walked to Janie's friend's unit. A quick look at Zack's stern face told her he was doing the same thing.

"Based on what we have right now, I think these are crimes of hatred. Personal hatred," Carlee ventured. "Like they're marking the victims as being two-faced, maybe? Making them ugly on the outside to match the inside, according to the killer's perspective?"

Zack hummed. "Maybe. But there aren't strong personal links between any of the victims beyond career field."

"Fine, let's focus on their field," Carlee said. "We need to draw up some theories about why someone would target beauty industry up-and-comers. These killings could be a statement... or revenge."

"It's revenge." Zack's expression darkened like a storm. "Which is why I'm damned near positive that we're after a man. Not a guy with opinions on makeup—just some pathetic asshole who was ignored or rejected by these women."

On the surface, Zack's theory seemed plausible, though there was one thing he'd missed.

"The lack of sexual assault makes me hesitant to chalk this all up to some generic, woman-hating serial killer," she said. "There are still too many unknowns to start guessing the killer's gender."

Zack's neck reddened with disgust. "More often than not, murders like this are the work of a lone wolf loser who thinks women owe him their time and their bodies. Never mind that these guys are shut-in assholes with no desirable traits or basic hygiene. In their minds, it's always women's fault. I've seen it thousands of times, Carlee... more than I want to remember. More than I *can* remember."

She sighed. "I suppose. I've run into my fair share of creeps, but that doesn't mean *this* murderer is one of them. We have to be careful not to narrow our suspect list down too much with guesswork."

They finally reached the door they were looking for, and Zack rapped his knuckles on it. A young woman poked her head out, swiping chestnut curls away from dark eyes.

"Hey, we're really sorry to bother you like this," Carlee began, her usual polite spiel. "Are you Kinzie Patel?"

"I am," she confirmed, looking nervous and like she hadn't slept for days. "Can I help you?"

"I hope so. I'm Carlee Knight—the private investigator who called earlier," she said. "And this is Detective Zack West."

"We have some questions about Janie Toland," Zack added.

"Oh, yeah, of course." Recognition flashed across Kinzie's face, like she had forgotten their hours-old conversation already. "My bad, Miss Knight. I've been really scatterbrained since..." She flinched. "Well, you know. Please, come in."

Kinzie retreated into her apartment, leading Carlee and Zack into her living room. In stark contrast with Kinzie herself, the room was bright and expertly decorated in floral patterns and art prints.

A quick peek into the open bedroom as they passed by revealed Kinzie's true state: a messy bed, sheets tousled and pillows flung about, clothes in piles on the floor, and a collection of half-empty cups and plates with mostly untouched takeout containers.

Kinzie's gaze drifted between Carlee and Zack. "So, what is it you wanted to ask me? What do you need to know about Janie?"

"We were hoping you could give us a better idea of who she was," Zack said. "It might help us find her killer."

"Makes sense," Kinzie said, but a long, wheezy sigh chased her words. "Go ahead."

"Could you start by telling us how you knew her?" he asked.

"Yeah, of course. I work at the Demode Vintage Salon, so—"

"You're not enrolled at Aphrodite?" Carlee interjected.

Kinzie didn't seem to mind the interruption and shook her head. "No. I used to be, but I graduated years ago. Janie did some work as a model, and I saw her once or twice at the salon."

"And that's how you met her?"

"Yeah. You have a lot of time to chat when you're cutting and styling and all that, so we got to be friends that way."

Carlee gave a thoughtful hum. "When did she decide she wanted to attend Aphrodite?"

"See, Janie was smart," Kinzie said. "She knew she had a shelf life as far as modeling went. She *also* knew how well I get paid, and she started asking me about the job. I told her if she was serious, she should go to Aphrodite and learn from the best." Kinzie smiled, though it was a pained smile, shuttered behind the tint of happy memories. "And that's what she did."

"What was her specialty?" Zack asked, more to keep Kinzie talking than to uncover some precious secret.

"She was going in for cosmetology."

"Was she any good?"

"Oh, yeah! Janie was a maestro with minimalistic makeup looks. One of the best I've ever seen. She was only getting better at the institute, except for... well...."

Carlee waited for her to continue, and when she didn't, gave her a verbal nudge. "Except for *what*, Kinzie?"

"It's just..." Kinzie glanced down at her hands, which couldn't seem to stay still in her lap. "We would talk a lot, and she spent most of that time trashing her instructors."

"Anyone in particular?"

"No." She looked reticent, not wanting to cast her friend in a negative light. "Not serious grievances or anything like that. Just normal venting stuff, you know?"

"Enlighten me," Zack said. "Normal stuff like what?"

"Some of the instructors have..." Kinzie tapped her chin, frowning, looking for the right term. "Well, they have what you might call 'classic' tastes."

"Outdated?" Carlee parsed Kinzie's polite words.

"Old as dirt?" Zack tried.

"You said it, not me," Kinzie protested, fighting down a weak grin. "Anyway, Janie could be abrasive if you didn't know her. She was critical of everything. But it's school, right? You're supposed to be frustrated with every little thing about school. I know I was."

"Did she vent like that with her classmates?"

Kinzie shrugged. "She might have."

"You think it earned her any enemies?" Carlee asked.

Kinzie lifted her brows and blinked. "She was a little bitchy. I mean, I'm sure some of the others hated her, but not enough to kill her. It was just some shitty, snobby trash talk."

Kinzie stood up and walked to a counter filled with photos, plucking one from the crowd. She smiled sadly at it before returning to hand the frame to Carlee—a picture of Kinzie and Janie at a bar, beaming, their arms around each other's shoulders.

"Does that look like the kind of person who could make somebody so mad they'd want to kill them?" Kinzie asked, sitting back down.

It was hard to disagree with her, though Carlee knew all too well how easy it was for a skilled liar to hide her true self. It's what she'd been doing practically her whole life after all.

Carlee passed the photo to Zack. "Kinzie," she said, "I'm sorry to be curt, but I want you to know I'm genuinely just trying to get the full picture of what happened to your friend. I need you to be honest with us, so please tell me the truth. Did Janie use any illicit drugs?"

Kinzie leaned back in her chair, suddenly looking apprehensive.

"Janie doesn't need you to protect her now, Kinzie," Zack said in a surprisingly gentle tone. "She can't get in trouble, and we aren't trying to disparage her memory. We're only interested in finding her killer."

Kinzie squeezed her eyes shut and dropped her face into her hands. She sighed.

"Yeah, she did. Though as far as I know, it was only sometimes. She wasn't an addict or anything like that." It was obvious that she didn't relish revealing these details, like she was posthumously betraying her friend.

"Do you know what drugs she used?" Carlee asked.

"Mostly weed. She tried coke once but hated every second of it. Said it made her spazzy."

Carlee logged that away, mentally rifling through conflicting theories. Ketamine was a heavy choice for someone who only smoked pot. Still, it didn't eliminate the possibility that Janie had casually dipped her toe into something harder that night, and her attacker saw an irresistible opportunity. Maybe they'd even offered her the ketamine. If Carlee could find the source of Janie's drugs, she might find her killer.

"Do you know who her dealer was?" Carlee pushed. Realizing she was leaning forward in her chair, she forced herself to straighten back up.

"I don't, no."

"Do you know where they do business? Anything else about them?"

THE TWO-FACED KILLER

Kinzie glanced down like she couldn't bear to see the disappointment on their faces. "I don't. Janie was tight-lipped about... that. She didn't want to let me in."

"Are you sure, Kinzie?" It was a believable story, yet the speed with which Kinzie answered made Carlee think she was hiding something. "This could be pivotal to our investigation."

"I'm being honest. I told you she smoked weed, didn't I?" Kinzie insisted. Again, a hair too fast for Carlee's taste.

"You know, my stylist complains that her work is too stressful all the time," Carlee said, hoping her hair looked good enough to give credence to the lie that she had a stylist in the first place. "She handles a ton of clients every day, and she says that the higher-end they are, the more demanding they are."

Kinzie's posture relaxed. "You don't know the half of it!"

"She told me the only way she manages is with a little chemical relief. I don't blame her, considering some of the meltdowns I've heard her deal with in the salon."

"I don't do drugs... if that's what you're asking."

"Oh, no! I just wondered if your salon is that stressful too?"

"I, um... I guess so?" Kinzie mumbled, eyeing Zack cautiously, even as she spoke to Carlee. "You get used to it, though. Most clients aren't too bad if you know how to distract them."

Glancing over at Zack, Carlee saw that he had sensed it too. Kinzie was going cagey, her words trailing off as her breath quickened. She was in the middle of a sloppy lie.

Kinzie's right hand instinctively tugged at the sleeve of her shirt. There was a daub of makeup smeared on the inside of the sleeve, and inspiration hit Carlee like a lead brick.

"I'm not drug enforcement," Zack assured her, holding up his hands in a calming gesture. "I'm only interested in finding Janie's killer."

"But if CPD *was* afraid her drug use could interfere with the investigation, they'd have to punt it over to Narcotics, of course," Carlee threw in, a hint of menace in her voice. Kinzie's eyes widened slightly. "Regulations, you see."

"Very true," Zack said, catching on to Carlee's little scheme. "But detectives are given a fair amount of discretion on what we need to report, especially when the witness is being helpful."

"Well, Kinzie?" Carlee prompted, closing in. "Are you going to be a helpful witness? Are you willing to help us catch Janie's killer?"

"I'm *trying* to help you, okay? I really am," Kinzie said, tears starting to well up on her lower lashes. "But if y'all are trying to catch Janie's killer, why do I feel like I'm on the stand all of a sudden?"

Time to pump the brakes. Carlee was still suspicious that Kinzie wasn't telling them everything, but she would be useless to the investigation if pushed past her limit. She backtracked as soothingly as she could.

"All we need is your cooperation. You're not on trial, and you're definitely not in trouble."

"If you say so." Kinzie sniffed, skeptical, staring at her tangled fingers in her lap. "It sure feels like I'm being interrogated."

Carlee was plotting where to steer the conversation, scanning Kinzie's room for any sign of personality she might use to lighten up the interview—an effort to calm their cracking source down—when she noticed a peculiar setup by Kinzie's computer.

The 4k webcam, the ring light, the streaming board—the telltale setup for every content creator on the internet.

"Hold the phone," Carlee murmured, putting on a shy smile and adopting a less formal, more juvenile style of speech. "You're not a streamer, are you?"

"Why?" Kinzie took a deep breath, carefully dabbing her face with the back of her hand.

"Because I was checking out your cam setup, and I'm jealous as hell. That's pro grade, girl! Where did you get that?"

"Oh, that's not mine." Kinzie's hunched shoulders relaxed as her expression smoothed over. "That's Janie's stuff. She did a makeup tutorial series that was kind of taking off, I guess?"

Zack's nose wrinkled with confusion—and a note of alarm. "What's all her gear doing over here?"

"Janie always filmed at my place because it's quieter. Better acoustics, she said. I don't really know much about recording."

Zack's mouth tightened, irritation creeping onto his face. Carlee could see he'd decided the interview had nothing left to offer, but she didn't share the feeling.

"Not to get way off track, but I've always wanted to start up a podcast," Carlee lied through her teeth. "I just can't seem to actually get started, you know?"

"I get it." Kinzie smiled, fragile but real. "Janie said the same thing until she finally ripped the Band-Aid off and started posting."

"How'd she get started?"

"Mostly technique videos, but then she branched off into product reviews, and that brought her numbers up, like, immediately," Kinzie said, her body language relaxing as Carlee's tangent distracted her. "She was hoping to become a full-time influencer."

"For sure! That's the dream, isn't it?" Carlee encouraged her to go on with a nod.

"I haven't watched the newer videos, but she was super excited about them. Said she got her hands on some top-of-the-line, really exclusive stuff." A cold look flashed behind Kinzie's eyes and she sat up straighter, as if chilled by her train of thought.

"What is it?" Zack asked.

"You don't think she might've pissed off a competitor or something, do you?"

Zack sighed. "I have a lot of thoughts about everything you've said."

He would wrap up the interview if Carlee couldn't get anything concrete soon, but to hell with Zack West, because *she* knew they were onto something big—she just needed to uncover it without pushing Kinzie over the edge.

Another glance around the room revealed a silver balloon statue on the top shelf of the bookcase behind Kinzie. Judging from the tiny engraving, it was an award marking a quarter of a million subscribers.

"No freaking way!" Carlee exclaimed, pointing at the award. "Is that a fan balloon?"

"Yeah. For Janie's channel."

"That's a huge deal! Her channel must have been crazy popular." Carlee did the mental math, calculating the height of the shelf compared to Kinzie, and determined it would be marginally out of her reach. Exactly what she needed to execute the brash plan cooking in her head...

"Sure is," Kinzie said. "Janie was totally over the moon about that. But she didn't even get a chance to do a special post about it." Grief flickered across her far-off expression, tugging the corners of her mouth into a stiff frown. "She was on track to get a gold balloon by the end of the year."

"That's amazing! Could I take a closer look at it? I've never seen one in person," Carlee gushed.

THE TWO-FACED KILLER 41

Kinzie, obviously puzzled but still desperate to prove herself helpful, immediately got up to retrieve it. The award was at the top of the bookcase, and she had to stand on tiptoe to try and reach it.

"Here." Carlee stood, tossing Zack a wink. "Let me help…"

She pretended to stumble as she approached, grabbing onto Kinzie's arm for support and peeling back the sleeve of her shirt, smudging the makeup she had seen earlier. With the foundation smeared away, several track marks lay thick and dark in the crook of her elbow—just as she suspected.

Kinzie dropped the balloon like it had burned her and pulled the sleeve back down, but Carlee had already seen the marks plain as day.

She looked back at Carlee, guilt crashing across her face. "I can explain."

"Kinzie, listen to me. I don't give a damn about the drugs," Carlee promised. Her heart panged for this girl. She hoped distressing her would be worth it in the end, after they brought the killer to justice. "All I care about is finding Janie's dealer."

If anything, Kinzie looked more afraid than ever. "It's not that easy," she stammered, shaking her head.

"It is," Carlee insisted. "Whatever you're scared of, we can protect you."

"No, you can't!" she shouted, her outburst startling Carlee back a step. "Y'all think you're looking for some smalltime pill lady, but you don't know the first damned thing about who you're dealing with!"

"Then tell us!" Zack boomed, choosing that moment to lose his patience. "You know something—so stop stalling and help us help you!"

Kinzie shrunk back in on herself, pulling her sleeves down as far as they would go. "I—I can't."

"Why not?" Carlee asked gently.

"Because she'll kill me!"

"Who is she?" Zack demanded, much less gently. "Who's going to kill you? Quit jerking us around and spit it out!"

"Look, Kinzie," Carlee cut in, pushing her way past Zack's blunt-force approach. "No one's going to kill you, but I *know* whoever killed Janie will murder someone else if we can't stop them. Are you going to be okay knowing you could've helped us and didn't?"

Kinzie bit her lip so hard, Carlee thought it might bleed. "God damn you," she finally relented, half laugh and half stifled sob. "You won't leave me alone until you get me killed, will you?"

"Nobody's going to kill you," Carlee promised. "Everything you tell us today will be completely anonymous. We're going to make sure no one else gets hurt."

"That only proves you're in way over your head. I *do* know who Janie's dealer is, and I know that neither of you stands a chance against her."

Carlee and Zack exchanged a glance, anxiously waiting in the heavy silence as Kinzie calmed herself enough to finally come clean.

"Janie's dealer... she's a queenpin."

"A what, now?" Carlee asked.

"See? You have *no* idea who you're up against. She's not just any queenpin. She's *the* queenpin," Kinzie breathed, with as much reverence as if she were speaking about actual royalty. "She rules with an iron fist, controls drugs in the industry both in Chicago and beyond. And she is *very* secretive. If she found out I told you about her..."

"A name, Kinzie," Zack pushed. "That's all I need."

"She doesn't have a name. She has a title." Kinzie's voice dropped to a shivering, worshipful hush. "She goes by the Duchess. And she's fucking untouchable."

Chapter Six

The wooden rolling chair creaked as Zack sat back. He took a deep breath and closed his eyes, mentally preparing himself to get to work.

It had been a few hours since he'd dropped Carlee off at her office. After arranging for an undercover car to sit outside Kinzie Patel's apartment for a few days, guaranteeing her safety—or at least a little peace of mind—they'd adopted a divide and conquer strategy to look into the fabled "Duchess," as Kinzie called her. By all accounts, she was a mythological fixture of the Chicago fashion and beauty industry. While plenty of wealthy patrons went to the Duchess for her access to top-of-the-line makeup, many young models, influencers, and artists were really after a cushier, safer drug experience than a typical dealer could offer.

Carlee had told Zack, in her usual cryptic way, that she could dig into the Duchess on her own—just to not ask her exactly how. He supposed he wasn't in a position to judge.

Plus, with all the shit he'd put Marisol through lately, letting an unauthorized private investigator into the CPD bullpen would probably not fly.

Even after the clever, if crude, stunt Carlee pulled at the apartment, Kinzie had never met the Duchess herself, and she still didn't know for sure if Janie had been in direct contact with her. All they knew was that Janie had dropped hints about an exclusive new dealer in the days before her death, bragging about the "boutique experience."

"Jesus Christ," he muttered. It all made Zack's head hurt. Scrubbing a hand over his face, he opened his eyes to the piles of photographs scattered across his desk.

According to his contact in Narcotics, the Duchess wasn't even on their radar. It was a damned good thing he liked a challenge.

Still, it brought Zack back to a problem that had been nagging at him since Kinzie's interview: why would any high-class dealer—in either makeup *or* drugs—want anything to do with a cosmetology student like Janie? It led him to conclude that Janie had lied to impress her friend, but even lies needed to be investigated.

So far, he had been going through all the information on Janie he could find, struggling to put together a profile that might help him suss out a more realistic dealer than the Duchess. He pulled up a picture that had run next to a newspaper article on the murder. It featured a younger Janie, still sporting braces, playing ball in a neighborhood park.

She seemed to have grown up in a low-income but relatively safe neighborhood—the exact type of place that Zack knew a particular class of dealer liked to set up shop. He was confident her old stomping grounds contained the key to finding Janie's actual dealer, and at the very least, it would provide a new, unvarnished perspective on her life.

Drugs usually loosened lips. If Janie had been stalked or abused by some misogynistic creep—and Zack felt increasingly sure that was the case—a chatty dealer might know about it.

He was rummaging for the toxicology report when he heard the unmistakable click of bootheels enter the room. Their tempo, their gait, and the sudden hush of the bullpen all pointed toward one person, so he scrambled to turn his Janie Toland intel facedown on the desk.

"Could you please tell me"—Marisol's voice landed on him like a weight—"why one of my detectives is busy haranguing another precinct for reports on a murder that isn't even ours?"

"I would be happy to, Commander." Using his boss's formal rank was an obvious ploy to soften her, but it only worked about half the time. Judging from the unimpressed set of her small, stern face, this was not one of those times. "I was just going to talk to you about that."

"Oh, you were, were you?" she said. It was only his near decade of experience that allowed him to smile despite her withering glare. "As I recall, I gave you two options, West. Work the Barclay case from your desk or take a few days off like the doctor told you."

The mention of the nasty whack to the head Todd McKinney, Carlee's last perp, had given him triggered the low, dull thud that had been present in the back of his neck ever since. The doctor had insisted he take some time off work, but there was too much to do. He knew the bruise must've looked bad; Marisol had even stormed into the hospital, demanding to see him, like a parent about to unleash her fury.

"I know, Commander, it's just—"

"And then I hear you were on the scene with that woman found wandering around in Millennium Park?" Marisol's eyebrows shot up, and her shoe sole tapped against the tile floor.

"I can explain."

"To me, it seems like a detective of mine—who has been given specific orders—is doing everything but what he's supposed to be doing."

"I know what it looks like," Zack said, holding his hands out, palms down. "But I was right down the street meeting a contact when the call came in."

Marisol chuffed. "How convenient."

"I was! I left my car there and ran to the park to see if I could assist. That's it."

"Uh-huh." Marisol leaned over and slid a blank folder off the top of his stack, revealing Janie's toxicology report. "And what's this? Some light reading?"

"You can't fault me for being curious. A force of professional habit," Zack said. He had never been very good at charm, but Marisol wouldn't have appreciated it anyway.

"I'd prefer you keep your professional habit focused on your assigned cases," Marisol shot back. "Lest I be forced to bring consequences down upon you."

"There isn't anything new with the Eighth-Grade Killer investigation," Zack protested. "Believe me when I say I hate the lack of leads, but what else am I supposed to do? Wait around until something new crops up?"

He began to shuffle through the files on his desk, trying to signal to his commander that they both had better things to do.

"About that. Time for you to refocus, curiosity and all"—Marisol's lip quirked the way it always did when she knew something he didn't—"because the CSU boys just lifted a partial print from one of Joel Barclay's buttons."

The files slipped from Zack's hands and onto the floor.

Chapter Seven

The figure lurking in the shadows, somehow darker than the darkness surrounding it, drew a glinting blade. Its prey, a beautiful, unsuspecting woman, was framed in the doorway. She had only moments left before the knife plunged into her. Violins began to trill.

"Okay," Carlee squawked. Her feet kicked out from under her on the couch, accidentally swiping at Alicia, who cried out dramatically. She snatched the remote and changed the channel.

"Hey!" Alicia squealed.

"I'm putting my foot down. We're not watching this shit."

The massive television screen that took up the majority of Carlee's living room wall went dark for an instant before flashing to a news channel. An inoffensively bland anchor was in the middle of an equally bland sports report.

Alicia booed, throwing her arm toward the screen in objection. "It was just getting good!"

Carlee glared at her, a forkful of carbonara halfway to her mouth. "If you thought that was good, I might have to schedule an intervention about your taste in movies."

"Come on, Carlee, you're killing me!" Alicia's grin was wide, barely holding back a laugh. "The demon was about to get her with the knife! That's classic cinema right there."

Carlee rolled her eyes and ripped off a chunk of garlic bread, dipping it in the sauce that had pooled at the bottom of her Styrofoam clamshell container. It was takeout night—Carlee's turn—and Alicia insisted on dinner and a movie. She would've slammed the door in her best friend's face had she known what movie she would pick.

"But that's the thing, Alicia," Carlee said. "Why on earth does a demon need a knife in the first place? Shouldn't it have, I don't know, claws or something?"

"It was a demonic knife, Carlee Knight. Were you not paying attention to the exposition?"

They fell into a fit of laughter, buoyed by delicious pasta and a good bottle of red wine. Their mirth was cut short when the newscaster pivoted to a second camera, the headline "Two-Faced Killer Returns?" emblazoned next to his face.

"We'll have the full report on the latest victim after the break," the anchor said, and the commercials rolled.

Carlee tried to keep up her smile, but it bled out, the realities of her life invading what had been such a pristine moment. To her credit, Alicia didn't try to undercut the tension with a joke or a jab.

"Um, not to dampen the mood, but... have you figured out who is sending you those creepy letters?" Alicia asked, brow furrowed with worry, concern in her eyes.

Carlee had been deliberately keeping the worst parts of the harassment from her, but she couldn't keep Alicia from noticing something was wrong.

"No, nothing new. Not really," Carlee lied, glossing over the little incident with the sheep's heart. "I think they've finally lost interest.

They probably hoped to send me to a psych ward by now and, since I'm still out and about, moved on to something else."

Alicia clicked her tongue, a look of profound disgust on her face. "Motherfucker should be in jail."

"Hey, no arguments from me."

Alicia took three angry bites of her risotto, and Carlee couldn't help but smile, though her guts were churning at the mere mention of her stalker. As expected, none of the security cameras outside her office had caught a glimpse of the person who'd delivered the heart, and despite what she'd told Alicia, Carlee had a hard time believing they were done with this sick game.

"And we're back to the story of the week," the TV anchorman said, addressing his viewers with a sober gaze. "There appears to be new information on the re-emergence of the Two-Faced Killer, an unidentified serial murderer who terrorized Chicago and its environs almost thirty years ago, attacking victims at—"

Carlee shut her eyes tight, willing the world to give her a moment's peace. When she opened them, the anchor and some talking-head "expert" were discussing the wandering woman. Coverage of Janie's murder had all but exploded. Newspaper headlines, old serial killer documentary reruns, nearly twenty-four-hour coverage from TV stations and social media... Everyone was losing their minds over the Two-Faced Killer's return. Worse, Carlee knew from her memories of Harborside that some people were *excited* rather than terrified.

After parting with Zack, Carlee had spent the rest of her day looking into leads on the Duchess. Following Kinzie's tip, she focused on luxury cosmetics brands—specifically boutiques.

Boutique makeup, boutique drugs, Carlee had thought as she pulled up website after website of Chicago-based cosmetic manufacturers, but her search yielded a dizzying number of results. She'd only ever used products grabbed off a drugstore shelf...

Carlee couldn't help but remember her mother tutting at her, holding out a fluffy brush and a palette of eye shadow, waving her preteen daughter closer. Her preference for burying her nose in a coding book or tinkering in the garage used to worry Mom, though she always nagged her with a smile.

"It's not difficult, Snapdragon. Imagine—Carlee Knight, tech-geek extraordinaire, scared of a little eyeliner!"

Later, Carlee had insisted. She always said later, until it was too late.

She shook off the unwanted memory and forced herself to page through the details of the case.

Carlee had keyed in on makeup community social pages and quickly found a consensus on the best—if not the most expensive—producer in the Chicagoland area: Facade by Jaq Curwood. It was a small company that specialized in limited edition, low-volume makeup lines. A cosmetics version of the crazy-popular sneaker drops that had been generating so much buzz.

Jaq Curwood's stuff was apparently so sought-after and so exclusive that it was nearly impossible to get without a personal connection, and even that didn't get you access to the top-of-the-line stuff. To get that, you had to be personally earmarked as a "promising up-and-comer" by the people at the top.

After some digging, Carlee discovered that the business owner wasn't "Jaq Curwood" at all, but some woman named Jasmina Callenwood.

She peeked over at Alicia, who somehow still looked perfect while sticking a forkful of risotto in her mouth. Carlee glanced down at herself, noticed carbonara on her t-shirt, and realized just how out of her depth she was in the world of makeup and glamour.

"Hey, Alicia." She chewed on her bottom lip. "Any chance you've heard of *Facade by Jaq Curwood*?" Carlee made sure to put as much panache onto the title as possible and was rewarded with a hearty laugh and bits of risotto landing on her coffee table.

"Yes, I have indeed heard of *Facade by Jaq Curwood*," Alicia said, mimicking Carlee's pronunciation. Then her eyes went wide. "Wait. Is Carlee Knight—*the* Carlee Knight, who once mistook my makeup sponge for birth control—asking me about makeup right now?"

"Damn it, how many times have I told you to quit bringing that up," Carlee grumbled, feeling like she had just opened Pandora's box. "I just have some ques—"

"Oh, yay! I have been waiting for this moment since we first met," Alicia said, her voice light with giddiness. "Give me two seconds, and I'll go grab my kit."

"What? No!" Carlee blurted, grabbing her friend's wrists to bring her back down to the couch.

Alicia's expression fell from pure excitement to crestfallen in a heartbeat. "Please, Carlee. Please let me put some makeup on you..."

Carlee remembered the look on her mom's face every time she told her *later*. "Er... give me a second before you go get it, and then you can do whatever you want to my face."

"Okay?" Confusion replaced Alicia's sadness, and she thankfully ignored what might have been Carlee's most painfully awkward sentence of the year. "But you're acting very, *very* weird right now, and if you tell me you really do want a makeover, I'm going to start suspecting you were body-snatched."

"I don't. Just one question, that's all."

"Shoot."

"What's so special about Jaq Curwood stuff, anyway?"

"I wouldn't know. I've never actually gotten my hands on it," Alicia said.

"But you have tons of products."

"I do, but not Jaq Curwood's."

"Why not?"

"Because it's hard to get. If a Jaq Curwood eyeshadow palette sells out—and they *all* sell out—you'll never see it again. And unless you're on their premium list, hooked up to be notified in advance, you won't even know it's available in the first place."

"Really? People go that wild for some dyed wax and eye gunk?"

"Like you wouldn't believe!" That earned Carlee the biggest eye roll she had ever seen. "People pay over a hundred dollars for Jaq Curwood eyeshadow palettes alone," Alicia said indignantly. "A lot of the influencers I follow love the stuff. Not a single negative review, or at least none I've seen."

"A hundred dollars for eye shadow?" Carlee exclaimed. "That's insane!"

"No arguments about that. Here, I'll show you." Alicia pulled out her phone, and soon, Carlee had a connection request to a video playlist titled "Makeup to Pick Up," a trove of product reviews Alicia had her eye on.

"Alicia, there are"—Carlee squinted at her phone and double-checked the number—"nearly a thousand videos in this playlist."

"I'm thorough. What can I say?" she sassed, pridefully primping her hair. "But it's been several seconds and *many* questions now, babe. What about the face you promised me?"

Carlee flinched. She was positive she had just committed herself to hours of obligation. Sighing like a prisoner resigned to torture, she gave a weak curl of her wrist, her most dramatic sign of consent. As Alicia pumped her fist and scurried across the hall to retrieve her makeup bag, Carlee cleared a spot on the coffee table between the garlic bread and wine glasses, plunking her laptop down.

She began clicking through the multitude of makeup videos marked *saved* and *viewed*. And before she knew it, one of the thumbnails on Alicia's favorites list caught her eye. It was an entire channel dedicated to Jaq Curwood products. The channel was relatively small, but the view count on its latest video was catching two to three times the subscriber number. She clicked, and as the title card faded away, a familiar face filled the screen.

Janie Toland.

Carlee's mind scrambled to catch up. She couldn't help but be impressed, if not a little baffled, by the production value of the video. Janie had several Jaq Curwood products arrayed in front of her and was meticulously going over each of them.

She was, to put it lightly, utterly scathing.

"This shit is *massively* overhyped," Janie said, slamming a container of what looked like foundation onto her vanity, letting the expensive powder explode out. And she didn't relegate it to a few bad batches, either. Janie was telling her audience that the whole Jaq Curwood brand was overhyped. She even brought up a screenshot of a drugstore lip gloss—one that Carlee was almost certain sat in her own bathroom—as a better alternative to the Jaq Curwood equivalent.

"Hey! Isn't this the girl who was just in the news?" Alicia asked.

"It sure is! When was this posted?" Carlee muttered, her gaze drifting down to the upload date. It was mere days before Janie had been found in the alley, dressed up and left in a pool of her blood.

If Janie had managed to get her hands on such an exclusive product—and thrashed it the way she had—she must've grabbed Jasmina Callenwood's attention. Maybe enough to wind up on the Jaq Curwood radar.

Maybe enough to wind up in an alley with her throat slit.

Chapter Eight

The steam from my usual mug wafted up from the kitchen table, the coffee's earthy aroma helping to alleviate this dismal mood. On a normal day, I would be turning the page of my daily newspaper, relishing the simple delight of print between my fingers. But here I was, scrolling through websites and search engines on a laptop I kept only by necessity.

It felt like selling out. Even in these small ways, I hated compromising my ideals.

Though I loathed foregoing my precious paper and ink, I had been clued in on something that promised to be worth it. An article had run recently in a newspaper I wasn't subscribed to. It contained something about the Eighth-Grade Killer. About me, and I *knew* Carlee had seen it.

And if Carlee had seen it, I wanted to see it too. I needed to see it.

I needed to know if she would make a move.

While my left hand scrolled through web text, my right hand twirled a newly acquired memento. I smiled as the printed logo of the Catty Corner Café swung in and out of view. But it wasn't the blue-ink logo that truly set it apart. It was the lipstick print along the cup's rim that made it so special to me.

The signature of Carlee's lips.

Her favorite coffee shop was hammy, not something I would've been caught dead in by choice, but its clientele was the best in Chicago. I'd been there a few times now, and on my most recent visit, I'd snagged this cup off the table an instant after Carlee and her detective friend rushed out of the establishment. They hadn't even remembered to tip, which told me more than words could say.

But their loss was my gain. It hadn't been hard to pluck the souvenir on my way out. The last dregs of Carlee's coffee had long since evaporated, leaving the bottom stained a murky brown. To her credit, at least she took her coffee black that day.

A few more clicks and I finally found it—the article. My anticipation rose as I read the title, "Don't Call it a Comeback."

"My thoughts exactly," I whispered. My blood seemed to sing at the headline's excitement. What a simple and pure way to encapsulate Joel Barclay—what he had given me, what he had given everyone. I simply wished the rest of the article had lived up to it.

My mood soured as I read and realized that the article was a general piece, not an ode to Joel. It was a hodgepodge of dated reportage about several different serial killers, none of them caught, including me. It didn't deserve half the attention it was apparently getting.

As if that wasn't enough, my blood boiled by the time I reached the end. The journalist—if they could really call themselves that—posited that my work with Joel had been the actions of a copycat.

Me? A copycat? I would never be a purveyor of artifice. I would never succumb to a performance without substance. There was little I reviled more.

My hot blood froze when I remembered Carlee had read this article. The credibility of my entire mission might be in jeopardy, I realized, clenching my fist atop the keyboard. I couldn't have her disbelieve the message I had sent to her by way of Joel's body.

It had taken so much *time* and *effort* and *planning* and *love*.

If I was honest with myself, in its most basic form, it was a love letter to Carlee.

A note to the sad, awkward girl all the other children had forgotten about, had not even considered, as they writhed and bled under my lights.

I can't imagine how lonely she must've felt, then and now. The message I sent was meant to be a way of reaching her, letting her know that she hadn't been forgotten. Joel had given his life to send that message, and now this petty newspaper journalist was trying to undermine it.

Carlee had seen it. I was sure of that. The article even mentioned her by name as one of the survivors of the *original* Eighth-Grade Killer, as if there were any other.

Did they succeed in throwing her off? Had she disregarded my love letter so easily? My promise? My threat?

I wanted—no—I *needed* Carlee to know I was out there, still waiting for her answer to my question. I couldn't have her walking around thinking that I was some *fake*. That I was somehow inauthentic. A facsimile, a ghost, of what I once was.

I *needed* her to dance to the tune that I set. If I was going to make her come to me, I needed to control her completely.

I reached for the clear orange tube seconds before the alarm on my phone went off. With a smile, I popped two pills into my mouth. A sip of coffee washed it all down. There was one good thing about constantly staring at my mortality, so starkly outlined and so poorly flavored; it was a constant reminder of the work I still had to complete. The pang of anger I felt each time I took a pill only motivated me.

And it was a reminder—a reminder that I didn't have time to sit around and wait for Carlee to understand my messages. I couldn't allow these writers to control the narrative. If I wanted my answer, I would have to push things along.

I twirled the paper cup one more time, took a peek inside, and saw some cold coffee still swirling at the bottom. I downed it, felt a visceral connection, and savored the stale flavor as I contemplated what would come for Carlee next.

I had just the idea.

I would have to send another message. A stronger message. And there was only one way the Eighth-Grade Killer sent messages.

Chapter Nine

The harsh halogen lights flared, trying their damnedest to blind her. Carlee and Zack had been in the halls of Aphrodite Institute for twenty minutes, but they only seemed to get brighter the deeper into the building they went.

The halls were stark—bone-white walls over bone-white vinyl tiling. For a place that was supposedly all about aesthetics, Carlee thought it was an odd choice. What she had seen so far reminded her more of a hospital than a beauty school.

But maybe that was on purpose. A student wouldn't be able to hide flaws in this barren sort of environment. It would also explain why the students gravitated to the front of the building, toward the windows and natural light.

"Who is this guy supposed to be?" Zack asked, trying to decipher one of the unclear maps dotting the walls. "And why are we meeting with him again?"

"Vinny Garrard. Office number A113," Carlee read off her phone, then shoved it back into her pocket. "And we're meeting with him because he's the closest thing Chicago has to a scientific expert on makeup and its composition. That I could find, anyway."

"Oh, right. The 'expert,'" Zack said snidely, then—ignoring Carlee's tired look—he opened up the file folder he was carrying and eyed a list of ingredients. "I'm going to test him... so he better know what 'Titanium Dioxide CI77891' is."

Carlee rolled her eyes. "Of course you are, Zack. Of course. You can only do that if we manage to find him, though."

She was keen to see if any of the ingredients used on Janie's body matched products sold by Jaq Curwood. If she could draw a connection, then perhaps a tie to Jasmina Callenwood might lead her to the enigmatic Duchess.

"Say, did you find anything on Jasmina?" Carlee asked. "Because I couldn't even find a parking ticket. If she's connected to the Duchess—hell, if she *is* the Duchess—her VIP clientele must be pulling some big strings for her."

"Maybe," Zack said, tilting his head from side to side, weighing the thought. "But I'd bet more on CNET not wanting to 'waste' resources on white-collar drug offenses."

"Really?"

Zack snorted. "Really. I wouldn't be surprised if they're turning a blind eye to it. In fact..."

"Carlee Knight?" a voice chimed from down the hall, interrupting whatever Zack had been about to say. "And you must be Detective West?"

The soft clatter of leather soles approached, and Carlee turned to see a man wearing a breezy linen shirt, capri pants, and a dazzling smile. With his perfectly coiffed hair and clear complexion, he managed to look stylish and full of vigor, even under the color-sapping, migraine-inducing lights.

"Is everyone in this building a model?" she whispered to Zack, suddenly aware of the abject plainness of her standard jeans and t-shirt.

Maybe she should have consulted Alicia about what to wear for her interview at Aphrodite. Even Zack, in his nice suit, looked remarkably pedestrian in contrast to the bright pastels and aggressive patterns walking toward them.

"You found us," Zack said, his rough voice bouncing off the clean walls and plain floor. "And I hope to god you're Vinny Garrard because we are completely lost."

"Not anymore, you're not." Finally reaching them, the man shook their hands enthusiastically. "I'm Vinny! And it is a pleasure to meet you both."

Two lefts, a right, a left, and two more rights, and Vinny led them into his office. Based on the extravagance of his dress, Carlee had been preparing herself for a room full of wild, ostentatious, over-the-top decor... something that shouted *style*. What she found when she walked through the door more closely resembled *high school guidance counselor*. Old, beige fabric chairs; white walls; a droopy, paneled desk; and a single—fake—plant.

"Welcome"—Vinny flared his hands dramatically—"to my kingdom."

"Huh," Zack said, voicing what Carlee was currently thinking. "Not exactly what I was expecting."

"You're not the first person to say that." Vinny flung himself into the office chair behind the sad desk. "But that's okay. I spend as little time in here as possible."

"You prefer being in the classroom?" Carlee guessed.

Vinny nodded, pursing his lips. "That or at my salon."

"You have a salon too?" Carlee gushed, pretending not to know.

"Sure. Most of the faculty at Aphrodite are working professionals. We do this because we want to give back to the community, teach the next generation."

"You don't look old enough to be worrying about the 'next generation' just yet," Zack said, making Vinny laugh good-naturedly. His smile didn't slip, but Carlee could sense a bitter backbone to the sound.

"I know I might not look it, but I have a head of grays under all this dye."

Picturing Vinny as a silver fox, Carlee had a hard time understanding why he wouldn't embrace that look with open arms—Zack was certainly making it work for him—but to each their own, she supposed.

"We're actually here to talk shop," Carlee said. "We understand you're an expert in the field of makeup."

Vinny's easy smile quickly turned upside down as he remembered why Carlee and Zack were visiting.

Zack handed the file over. "CPD Forensics was able to break down the chemical composition of the makeup found on Janie Toland, and we were hoping you might be able to give us some insight that could help with our investigation."

"Let's have a look." Vinny pulled a pair of reading glasses from the desk to review the list. Before long, he was clicking his tongue and muttering to himself. "These compounds at these levels—it's all fairly boilerplate as far as makeup goes."

"So...?" Carlee pushed for a clearer explanation.

"So, what you're looking at is almost certainly on the cheaper side. I would guess a generic pharmacy brand."

Not the hyperexclusive Jaq Curwood line. Carlee cursed inside her head. So much for her pet theory...

"Are you sure?" she asked, not quite willing to let the Curwood thread slip away. "There isn't anything to suggest it could be a high-end brand?"

"As sure as I can be," Vinny said. "Look, just because the product has a high markup doesn't mean it's worth the money—that's one of the first myths I have to break with a lot of my students. But you see here..." He pointed at a specific line on the list and tapped it as if his conclusion should've been obvious.

"Yellow 5 CI 19140?" Carlee read.

Zack crossed his arms. "It's what? A yellow dye?"

"Yes." Vinny clucked. "It was a very popular yellow dye with the higher-end lines three years ago. So popular, in fact, that the factories in Southeast Asia produced *far* too much of it, and the big players, as they always do, got bored and moved on. The generic brands picked up all the surplus and have been using it in everything ever since. You see it *everywhere*. It's a dead giveaway for low-end products."

Vinny flung out his hand to emphasize his point, but Carlee got the distinct impression he was pointing at *her* eyeshadow, which she had chosen specifically for this interview so as not to be dismissed out of turn. Now that she thought about it, the residue *did* have a slightly yellow hue when she'd brushed it off her fingertips that morning. Alicia told her to pick it because it was summery.

"All of this stuff"—Vinny swept his hand across the list—"is inferior quality. You could find this at the drugstore for three dollars."

"Five dollars," Carlee said under her breath, a little peeved. Zack gave her a side-eye.

"The point is," Vinny continued, "no self-respecting makeup artist would keep any of this in their bag, let alone use it, especially not on themselves."

"Well, that aligns with my 'misogynist killer' theory," Zack murmured, more for Carlee than for Vinny.

"What theory is that?" Vinny asked anyway.

"I think that the killer doesn't know anything about makeup. He just wanted to dress his victims up like cheap floozies because that's how he perceives them."

"We don't know any of that for sure," Carlee said, trying to put a lid on Zack's conjecture before he led their interviewee too far.

"You heard him, Carlee. If Janie was a talented student, she wouldn't buy or use the stuff found on her," Zack said, pointing at the list as if it were ironclad proof. "Which means our killer knows nothing about the beauty industry and bought it themselves. Didn't want to spend more than five bucks on it." He looked to Vinny as if hoping for backup, but Vinny merely glanced between the two of them nervously.

"Look, all we have right now are theories. So we can't rely on our *guts*," Carlee added pointedly, "especially not yours."

An awkward moment passed between them, and Carlee—with great difficulty—broke her staredown with Zack to address Vinny. "I know this may be a long shot, but did you happen to know her?

"Who?"

"Janie Toland? Was she in any of your classes?" She pulled up a picture of Janie on her phone, holding it out for Vinny.

He readjusted his reading glasses and leaned in. Then, after a nail-biting moment, he shook his head.

"I might've seen her around the school, I suppose," Vinny said. "There are a lot of students at Aphrodite, and as much as I'd like to, I can't know them all."

Carlee flipped to another photo, hoping a picture of Janie with a different hairstyle or makeup look might jog his memory. She kept flipping until Vinny suddenly gasped and snatched the phone from her hands.

"*Her*, I *do* know," he said, flipping the phone around. "That's Iris. Iris Livingstone. She is one of my students!"

Carlee turned the phone around and saw that it wasn't a photo of Janie he was pointing at.

It was the woman they'd found wandering in the park.

Chapter Ten

The day turned into a mad dash to find out as much about Iris Livingstone as possible. It was now clear that the killer was targeting Aphrodite students, and there was no time to waste—or the next woman would surely turn up dead, posed in an alley with a slit throat.

Carlee and Zack asked Vinny every question they could think of, hunted down Iris's records in the Aphrodite administrative office, and called her information in to the hospital so the staff could begin checking for medical info. Carlee had become an Iris expert in the roughly twenty-four hours since Vinny identified her.

Iris Livingstone appeared to be a super-student. In her midtwenties, she was taking night classes at Aphrodite and spent her days at a full-time nursing program. The students they interviewed described Iris as intelligent, talented, and, above all, driven. Vinny spoke about her as if Iris was the dictionary definition of *ambitious*. He said she would hound him with questions, and smart ones too. Not just the "what really is mascara?" type of garbage that some of his students asked him. She had in-depth questions about the origins of different techniques and the direction the industry was headed. He could tell she wanted to *understand* these things, that she wanted to be at the cutting edge.

A quick call to the nursing school and a few conversations with her second set of professors told a similar story. Iris was an intelligent, talented, and driven young woman who had a bright future ahead of her in medicine. Some of the professors had already pegged her as a shoo-in for the nurse practitioner program.

"So she's a superhuman," Zack had said matter-of-factly after Carlee hung up with the nursing school.

"I wouldn't go that far. Hitting the books hardly makes you superhuman."

"I did two straight semesters and a summer of full course loads back in college and it nearly killed me," Zack admitted. "I was so stressed, I wound up drinking so much after my last final that I nearly got cirrhosis. And this Iris Livingstone is going full-time in two programs and acing both? Is she a wizard?"

Carlee thought back to how rough some of her college semesters had been, then tried to imagine throwing a whole extra program on top of that. She shivered before conceding the point.

"What's strange to me is that not a single person we've talked to had anything bad to say about her," Carlee said. "Janie was a little bitchy, but everyone's just gushing about Iris. None of them even hesitated. Not the slightest sign of a lie."

"So how does a universally loved, hardworking student end up stumbling through a public park, an escapee of a serial killer?"

The question hung in both of their minds until Friday evening, when Carlee and Zack finally found a moment to visit the hospital, hoping to secure at least one or two answers to these questions.

Instead, they found Iris—still unconscious, still fighting for her life.

"And as I already said, her prognosis isn't likely to improve," Dr. Khalil repeated, going over Iris's records a second time at Zack's insistence. "She had a dangerous amount of ketamine in her system. The fact that she wasn't blacked out when you found her is the result of a very rare situation. A minor medical miracle, if you ask me."

Carlee looked at the unconscious Iris, an IV bag steadily dripping fluids into her system and a battery of medical machinery lined up next to her bed. She willed Iris to hold on, certain her testimony would lead to the apprehension of the Two-Faced Killer.

Iris had to survive.

"What kind of situation, Doctor Khalil?" Zack asked. "I spoke to some of my CNET contacts, and they say a dose that high usually knocks a person out cold, so how *was* she still moving?"

Khalil flipped the pages of Iris's medical record, turning his clipboard around to show them. "The minor miracle I told you about," he said, as though a PI and a cop were supposed to understand the medical jargon cluttering the sheet.

Carlee looked at Khalil, the clipboard, then back up to Khalil. Zack was silent beside her.

"Iris Livingstone has a metabolism defect that makes her resistant to drugs," Khalil explained, taking pity on their blank faces. "Her body burns them off at a much faster rate than usual, so normal doses feel like small doses to her, and large doses feel like normal doses."

"So, the large dose that Iris got didn't hit her as hard as it should have?" Carlee asked, looking to Khalil for confirmation that she'd understood correctly.

He nodded, though she was sure he had significantly dumbed down the explanation. "This metabolism defect is the only reason she wasn't knocked out, and likely the only reason she got away."

"Do you think she's going to make it?" Zack's voice tightened an octave and his brow rumpled fiercely. "You said her body minimized the ketamine's effects, so why is she in such bad shape?"

"The ketamine isn't the problem," Khalil snapped, clearly not appreciating Zack's accusatory tone. He set the records aside and shot a worried glance at Iris, the rhythmic EKG machine filling the tense silence. "Our initial testing found that nearly all of Iris's organs are on the verge of failure."

"*Failure?* Is there something chronically wrong with her besides the metabolism thing?" Carlee asked.

"What do you mean?" Zack demanded, eyes narrow. "What do you think caused it, then?"

Khalil sighed. "Iris is a heavy-duty drug user. We found traces of multiple narcotics in her system. Mostly speed, but plenty of other things too. Her overactive metabolism probably caused her to take larger doses of everything, which is why her vitals have slowly been deteriorating. I hate to be so blunt, but... I wouldn't hold my breath for her to pull through."

"I guess that explains her academic schedule," Carlee said grimly, willing down the bubbling in her stomach before it could make her properly sick. "But I really need her to wake up. I have to know what she saw..."

"Not to be vulgar," Khalil said, scanning the hospital hallway for eavesdroppers, "but if this were a prop bet in Vegas, I'd advise you not to put money down on a good outcome. She isn't likely to regain consciousness."

"Have you informed her family?" Carlee asked, her heart rending as she stared at the poor girl in the hospital bed. Intelligent, talented, driven, an addict—and soon to be dead.

Khalil nodded. "We have, but they're all out of state. They'll try to be here, but with the condition she's in, there's no guarantee they'll see her before she passes."

Carlee and Zack exchanged pained looks. Iris represented their best bet of catching the killer, and even foggy details about her attacker could've been the difference between a swift end to the manhunt and another dead victim. To have a break in the case so close and yet so far away was maddening.

The injustice of it all was sickening. Iris had survived something truly terrible, had gotten herself to safety, and still might not live. It wasn't justice, and it wasn't fair, and worst of all—there was nothing, absolutely nothing, Carlee could do about it. It made her head spin and her thoughts turn red.

"Thanks, Doctor," Zack said, pulling Carlee out of her head. "Please let us know if anything changes or if she wakes up." He handed Khalil a business card, which he pocketed with a somber nod.

"Will do. But like I said, don't get your hopes up." Khalil stepped away to attend to his other patients, leaving Zack and Carlee in Iris's room, the sound of ventilators and heart monitors performing a medical symphony—or maybe a dirge.

Carlee walked up to Iris, a woman she had never properly met—might never meet—and held her hand.

"What are you thinking?" Zack asked quietly.

"A lot of things," she said without turning back to look at him. "Not least of which is how cosmically unfair all of this is."

"I agree. Unfair for her and for Janie," Zack added. "It's the toughest part of the job."

Carlee nodded, watching Iris's chest slowly lift up and drop down, willing her to get better. She was on the knife's edge of life and death.

In a blink, Carlee was back in her mother's study, watching Mom drift in and out of pain, praying she would get a little more time with her.

Another blink and Carlee was back in the hospital. She took a deep breath, squeezed Iris's hand again, and turned to Zack.

"Come on. I'll walk you back to your car," he said softly, as if he might disturb Iris from her rest. "Not much else we can do here until she wakes up."

"*If* she wakes up."

"*When* she wakes up," Zack said defiantly. "I can tell. She's a fighter. She'll wake up."

Carlee wished she had his confidence. They walked back to their cars in silence. Zack said he'd contact her later to review the next day's investigation game plan and drove off. She watched him leave before getting into her own car.

Sitting in the driver's seat, the key unturned in the ignition, she thought about Iris. The parking lot was dark outside the islands of light cast by the few isolated lamp posts.

She had only been there for a minute when her phone rang. The caller ID revealed her father's familiar goofy smile. Should she even take the call? She certainly didn't feel like talking to anyone right now, but slid the bar to answer it anyway.

"Hey, Snapdragon!" Dad's cheerful voice rang from the speakerphone in stark contrast to Carlee's mood. It gave her emotional whiplash. "How're things going in the big ol' Windy City?"

Carlee was unsure how to respond, her mouth opening and closing. Eventually, she settled on, "Windy, I guess."

There was a moment of silence, and Carlee realized he was waiting for her to ask a question of her own. She hastily added, "How's Harborside?"

"Oh, you know." Dad sidestepped the awkwardness in a way only dads could. "Harbory."

She could hear the dumb smile on his face through the telephone and couldn't help but smile herself. But something was off. Dad shouldn't be this jovial. She had ducked out on dinner at least twice in the past couple of months, which usually earned her stern, paternal reprimands, not his top-shelf dad jokes.

"About dinner," she started, figuring she would head off the fight at the pass.

"Don't worry about it, Carlee," he interjected. "Catherine and I both know how busy you can be."

"I know, but I'm still sorry. I really am looking forward to seeing you again."

"Well, then, you're going to love this! We're coming into Chicago next week!" he announced. There it was, the reason he wasn't mad. If she wouldn't come to him, they would come to her, and there would be no duck-outs or excuses.

"Whoa, there! Next week?" Carlee asked, going into fight-or-flight mode.

"Yeah! We have a whole trip planned. So, clear your schedule and—"

"You can't just drop that on me, Dad. I'm in the middle of a big case; there's no way that'll work. I could do next month, I guess?"

"But I thought you were hoping to see me again."

"I am, but..." Carlee dug the heel of one hand into her forehead. "Please, Dad. Please don't make me feel bad about this."

"I'm not trying to make you feel bad. I'm trying to spend some time with my daughter."

Carlee sighed. "Just let me finish this case and I promise we'll set something up, okay?"

"Okay, then next month!" he said quickly, no enthusiasm lost. She felt as if she were standing in a used-car lot and the dealer had just swindled her. "It's a date, Snapdragon. And no backsies this time. We're making reservations right now. Setting it in stone."

"Oh, wait. Did I say next month?" Carlee pinched her nose, tapping her finger on her steering wheel. "Can we put a pin in this, Dad? This new case is huge, and I'm not sure when I'll have it wrapped up."

"Oh." The smile finally disappeared from his voice. "Well, if that's the case, I guess—"

Images of Iris alone in the hospital bed, her family miles away, flashed in Carlee's mind.

"You know what, Dad? I can figure something out. Let's have dinner next week."

"Really?" he asked hesitantly. "We don't want to be a bother."

"You won't be, I promise," Carlee insisted. "There's a new Thai place I think you would like."

"Thai? You think Catherine would like it? You know she can't handle spicy."

"I know. They've got some mild dishes Catherine will like."

Or at least less spicy dishes, Carlee thought as a devious smile etched into her lips. She could handle Catherine for an evening, but watching her sweat and down cups of yogurt sauce would make it worth it.

"That sounds great, Snapdragon," he said, his high spirits back. "It's a date!"

"I'm looking forward to it."

Carlee said her goodbye and hung up. It was funny how a simple conversation with him could make or break her mood.

"Let's put this day to rest," she muttered to no one. She was just about to turn the key in the ignition, when—*rap rap rap!*—a hand reached out of the darkness and knocked on her window.

Carlee nearly launched herself through her roof and scrambled over the center console to the passenger seat. Framed in the window was the dark silhouette of a person, cloaked in night.

She wanted to yell or scream for help, but Carlee was silent, frozen with fear.

Chapter Eleven

Carlee's blood thumped in her ears. Her hands scrabbled for purchase on something, anything in her car that she could use to defend herself. Her whole body pulsed with fear.

"Open up!" The figure knocked on the window again. Their voice—*her* voice, Carlee realized—was tentative, and its tone gave her pause.

Abandoning her frantic grab for the umbrella in her back seat, Carlee reached up and flicked on the cabin lights, illuminating the mysterious woman just enough to reveal her face.

"Sharon?" Carlee gasped, relief crashing down on her. She scrambled to open the driver's side door. Sharon Campbell—the mother of her only childhood friend, Addison—politely stepped aside to let Carlee climb out.

"My god, I didn't mean to frighten you like that. Are you all right, Carlee?"

"I'm... I'm... What are you doing here?" Carlee flinched, hoping the question didn't sound accusatory. Relief spiraled quickly into a softer brand of dread, one mixed with a hefty helping of guilt.

Ever since the Eighth-Grade Killer's reign of terror, Sharon's unwavering kindness throughout the years had only strengthened Carlee's belief that Addison—the beautiful, popular, lively girl everyone in Harborside had loved—should have survived in her stead. Not dour, tongue-tied, geeky Carlee Knight, the girl almost nobody would have missed.

"I tried to call you." A bright smile spread across Sharon's freckled face. "But you must've been caught up with work or something because you never called me back."

"That's, um... right. I'm a little busy these days. But I'm really glad to see you! What brings you to the city? How did you know to find me here?"

"Oh, I didn't expect to see you at all. I just spotted you when I got out of my car. A family friend is in the hospital—nothing too serious—so I dropped by to see them. What an absolute delight to run into you... though I wish it had been somewhere else."

Carlee fumbled for a response, but only managed a weak smile. Talking with Addison's mother, the walking embodiment of survivor's guilt, was always difficult. And now Carlee was struggling with the added stress of having just had the piss scared out of her.

Get it together, Carlee, a voice that sounded suspiciously like Eleanor's shouted in the back of her head.

Her struggle must've been obvious because Sharon reached out to lay a hand on Carlee's shoulder. "What's wrong, dear? You look so pale..." A brief flash of worry crossed her face and she looked back at the hospital doors. "You're not sick, are you? My god, it's not Joseph, is it? Is your father okay?"

Carlee quickly waved off the concern. "No, no. He's fine. It's just..." She took one long, deep breath, resting a hand on the car door to steady herself. "I'm sorry I've been so hard to get ahold of, Sharon. I've been worried about work and everything else... but I'm fine. My father's fine too. I'm here on a work-related matter."

As Carlee's fight-or-flight reaction drained away, her brain grew the bandwidth to critically assess the situation. Sharon just so happened to be at the same hospital at the exact same time? What was she really doing there? And if visiting a family friend wasn't the real reason, why would she lie?

As she eyed Sharon up and down, guilt swept over her.

Eleanor's critical voice drifted into Carlee's mind again, reminding her that Sharon Campbell was one of the few people in Harborside who had always been civil to her. It was true. Even while the Campbells were mourning the loss of their daughter, and even when so many others in Harborside treated Carlee poorly, Sharon had been a steady comfort. To this day, she still sent Carlee handwritten birthday cards with carefully drawn hearts. Why on earth was she trying to find something suspicious about this woman?

Maybe Eleanor was right. Maybe she *was* running herself into a paranoid episode.

"From your shocked expression, I take it you didn't get my message?" Sharon asked gently, her smile widening as if to reassure Carlee she wasn't angry.

Carlee slowly shook her head, the tenderness making her feel even worse. A cowardly part of her *wished* Sharon would yell at her, scorn her, and refuse to speak to her again. It would be easier to completely abandon Harborside if everyone back home could finally agree that they were better off without the Knight girl, the one who shouldn't have survived, constantly reopening their wounds.

Carlee sighed. "I'm so sorry, Sharon. I should've called you back. I should've found the time."

"That's okay." Sharon waved off the apology as if it were nothing, but there was an odd expression on her face. Was it concern? Was it pain?

"How long are you going to be in Chicago?" Carlee asked, hoping to steer the conversation into less awkward waters.

"Not long, though I actually didn't call just to tell you I'd be in town," Sharon said, her hesitance to continue signaling that whatever came next was going to be uncomfortable.

Crap. No luck making things less awkward... but when had Carlee Knight ever managed to pull that off?

"Oh, uh... What did you want to...?"

"I called because... well, I saw that horrible article. The one about serial killers making 'comebacks,' or whatever it was. As soon as I saw the disgusting headline, I thought of you."

Carlee grimaced. "Oh, right, *that* article. Yeah, I saw it too. Some people are truly messed up in the head."

"That's putting it lightly," Sharon said, her voice hardening with each word. "I read it. I didn't want to, but I had to make sure they didn't say something terrible about my Addison. Then I..." She sucked in a sharp breath. "I saw your name."

Carlee leaned back against her car and dragged a hand over her face. So that's what this was about... "Yeah, well, if it's any consolation, I know how you feel. That damned writer had some, uh, 'colorful' things to say about—"

"You didn't help them write it, did you, Carlee?" Sharon blurted, a screw of pain tightening her face.

"Hell no!" burst out of Carlee's mouth before she could control the shiver that ripped up her spine. "Jesus, Sharon. Absolutely not. I've never—"

"Ever since that article came out," Sharon said, rubbing her arms as if to ward off a shiver of her own, "people have been hounding me. Calls at all times of the day and night, emails, all asking for interviews about the worst year of my life. Someone actually came to my house the other day and tried to pitch an Eighth-Grade Killer 'web series' or something to me. Not even a series for Addison, for the victims. It was going to be all about... that monster." The very idea that Carlee had been involved with that article put Sharon on the verge of tears. Her hand shot out to grab Carlee's, and she had to work hard not to instinctively jump back. It wasn't an aggressive move, just one made of misery by a still-grieving mother, desperate to be reassured that she hadn't been betrayed.

Carlee tried to think of something adequate to say.

A small part of her couldn't help but feel that she *was* responsible for the article and the grief it had caused Sharon. If she *hadn't* recently rattled Harborside with recent investigations, and then drudged up the Eighth-Grade Killer investigation in her wake, maybe that story never would have been published.

"I swear I had nothing to do with that garbage," she finally said. "I was as horrified as you were when I read it! Those people are twisted—completely twisted. And if I could do something to shut them up, believe me, I..." The air seemed to seep from her lungs before she could say anything better.

"You know what, Carlee? I'm—I'm sorry. Forget I brought it up. I don't know how I could even consider the possibility you had something to do with that," Sharon stammered. Then, before Carlee could protest, she drew her into a fragile hug. Carlee let it happen, and more than that—she reciprocated.

Sharon patted her back with the stiff, bracing taps of a midwestern mother. It felt entirely unlike her own mother's hugs, but then again, it had been so long since she died, Carlee wondered if she truly remembered the feeling of Mom's embrace.

Sharon released her, and one last shiver of dread ran through Carlee as she realized: the only reason there had been no immediate media blowout on her end was that Eleanor must've been screening her calls. How many amateur documentarians had tried to get ahold of her in the past few days? How many idiot serial killer bloggers?

The fact that Sharon had to go through any of it—especially due to a terrible, tasteless article with a cutesy rap-style headline—was unconscionable to Carlee. She wanted to hunt those people down and throttle them with her bare hands.

Sharon let out a long breath through her nose and closed her eyes. She relaxed a little, but it was only a veneer of relief. Judging from her tight shoulders, Sharon's tension still ran deep.

To see her so freshly upset after being accosted by vultures and click-seekers—a whole thirteen years after Addison had been killed—drove home the fact that this quest to catch the Eighth-Grade Killer wasn't only to put Carlee's fears to rest. It wasn't even just about getting justice for Addison and Cameron. The entirety of Harborside lived in the killer's lingering shadow. There were dozens of families affected by the Eighth-Grade Killer's spree, people who would never know peace until the murderer who stole their loved ones was taken down.

Carlee reached out and cupped Sharon's shoulder, not knowing what else to do in the awkward silence.

"I really should have called you back, Sharon. I'm sorry I didn't. And *next* time," Carlee swore, forcing a smile, "I will."

The dull light from Carlee's car lit up Sharon's smile, sad and wan. She nodded and squeezed Carlee's hand one last time.

"Well," Sharon finally said, giving a halfhearted shrug as she seemed to remember they were standing in a hospital parking lot. "I should probably get back to my friend. Maybe we could *plan* a little catch-up outing instead of playing phone tag and bumping into each other at a depressing place like this."

Carlee's stomach dropped. "That would be smart."

"Coffee or dinner, perhaps?"

"Both sound great," Carlee lied. "The next time you're in Chicago, give me a call—and I'll actually answer it!" *Nailed the landing there...*

"I'll see you soon, dear." Somehow, Sharon didn't seem to mind the awkwardness, or at least had the good graces to look past it. She gave Carlee one final hug before heading back into the hospital.

As far as unexpected conversations with people who filled her with self-loathing went, Carlee supposed that one wasn't so bad. But even if it didn't leave the aftertaste of despair in her mouth, it still made her wonder if she was wasting her time on the Two-Faced Killer case. Sharon's grief was a stark reminder that Addison's killer was still out there, and had possibly started killing again.

That pain Carlee had seen in Sharon tonight, undoubtedly just the tip of the iceberg, would be there until the Eighth-Grade Killer was no more.

Her thoughts were interrupted by another phone call, and the caller ID sent her already frayed nerves grating again.

Ian Garnett. Perfect fucking timing.

"If you're calling to insert yourself into my investigation," she answered before he could get a word in, "don't."

"Not this time. I'm afraid it isn't anything like that," Ian said, his voice severe and steely.

"So what *is* it like?" she joked, forcing herself to churn her anxiety into humor, the only way she knew to cope with the warning sirens going off in her head.

"I need to meet with you to discuss a private matter." He completely ignored her teasing, which did nothing for Carlee's nerves. "As soon as your schedule permits."

"A private matter?" she asked, confusion mixing with her unease. "Okay, now I'm really curious. Can you at least tell me what it's about?"

"I've learned something about your new henchman..." Ian paused as if to choose the right words. "Something disconcerting."

Carlee's mouth bent into a skeptical frown, her nose wrinkling. "Henchman? Are you talking about Zack?"

"Yeah. You're going to want to hear this, but it's not something I should say over the phone."

Carlee squeezed her eyes shut. "Ian, I don't need high school theatrics. Just tell me."

"I'd love to. Can you meet me first thing tomorrow?" No flash, no teasing, no smile behind the words.

"Tomorrow?" Not quite recovered from her encounter with Sharon, Carlee felt a chill run through her once again. She opened her eyes.

"And I mean it, Carlee," he said. "The sooner the better."

Chapter Twelve

My usual spot was taken. I had to park across the road, closer than I liked, and on the wrong side of the streetlamp I so often stood under to take my medication. I fought off a flare of anger, but then I realized it was probably for the best. Parking my car in the same place each time only made me easier to spot.

Not that Carlee would've spotted me. She hadn't so far. It was disappointing, a fact that suggested—to my great horror—she was no cleverer than the rest of Harborside. But I shook the notion away as soon as it bubbled up. My little rising star, as oblivious as she sometimes acted, was special.

She had to be special. It's why she was spared. If she *wasn't* special—then what was it all for?

As if my worries had summoned her, Carlee bustled out of her building's front door, a hapless mess—some sort of pastry in her mouth, still shoving her laptop into her bag as if she was physically incapable of stopping. As if she were a shark who would suffocate if she stopped swimming, even for a second.

I let out a deep, long sigh as she reached her car and haphazardly threw everything in. It all looked so amateurish.

My little shark found her bearings, then I watched her drive off. Even though it was the weekend, the bag filled with equipment meant she had left for work—which I knew for certain, because Carlee had all of her groceries and sundry day-to-day items mailed directly to her, like a shut-in. I also knew she would be gone through the evening, toiling away on her latest piddle-paddle investigation.

This gave me a nice, long window to prepare. I'd been observing my target for days now, planning out the perfect abduction. I certainly didn't want to feel rushed.

I waited ten minutes after her car disappeared down the street. The last thing I wanted was for everything to be thrown into the air simply because Carlee had forgotten something, and she had all the markings of someone who constantly forgot things.

My fingers began to tap on the steering wheel. I'd picked no particular beat or rhythm, but I could feel my hands start to move to one nonetheless—something original, bestial but reserved, like a jungle cat lying in wait. I liked it.

When the rhythm was all tapped out, I got out of my car and crossed the street. I approached Carlee's condominium casually, with the breezy stroll of someone who had lived there for decades. You didn't last as long as I had by *prowling*.

The anticipation had been thrumming through my veins for days. I was close now. So close, I could almost taste it on the back of my tongue. This stage of the plan was the most tenuous, the most exciting. All I needed to do was execute it—something I'd done many times—and I'd be well on my way to finding the answer to my Carlee Question.

My present goal was reconnaissance. I needed to double-check that I'd found all security cameras and exits around the building before the next phase commenced. It was easy enough. I simply needed to walk tall, smile quickly at anyone who passed by, and look like I belonged.

Today, there was no need to wear a hat or glasses, and certainly not a mask. I could hunt in my own skin.

My foray was a swift success. Another security camera had been installed in addition to the two at the front and back of the building, right above their respective exits. Rather bland and easy to bypass. There was another pair in the parking garage, mounted obviously on the support pillars, more for deterrence than surveillance.

The four tiny motion-activated pieces set up around the building's blind spots, though? *That* was doubtless Carlee's work. They added an interesting wrinkle but their coverage wasn't perfect.

I wondered if the building superintendent had ever taken down Carlee's handiwork—if they'd found her "improvements" and considered them a violation of other residents' privacy. I imagined they had a much harder time of it than I did.

My reconnaissance complete, I rounded the building and slipped through the front door.

The lobby was quiet, its impeccable white tile stacked with a few strategically placed palms, splays of lively green to break up the wannabe-chic Uptown monotony. I couldn't quite put my finger on why, but I felt my blood pressure begin to rise.

This was the place Carlee had decided to call home. This was where she had run away from Harborside to live. I couldn't help but feel even more disappointed.

Across the entry wall were the labeled mailboxes, and I found the one I wanted quickly enough. I knew exactly when my target would come home, exactly when I should expect her. As I traced my fingers along the name, my disappointment was drowned out by my pulse.

That familiar excitement was like a drug, but so much better and far more addicting.

This was my second favorite part of the process. Knowing what was coming but being forced to control myself, to keep myself on a tight leash, only heightened everything I felt.

It was starting again. The world would relearn the lesson it had been taught countless times before. If everything went as planned, she wouldn't even know I had been in this building, stood in this lobby... at least not until the precise moment I wanted her to know.

Not until she received my message. By then, though, it would be far too late.

Chapter Thirteen

Carlee was tempted to keep driving. She was fairly certain Ian hadn't seen her yet, and if she pressed her foot into the pedal, she could roll right by and pick up a coffee at Catty Corner. Anything to put off dealing with Garnett's typical FBI dramatics this early in the morning.

He was standing on the sidewalk outside her office building, waiting for her, because of course he was. She was sure the only reason he hadn't stormed up to her car was that he had his face buried in his phone.

Carlee let out a long, deep sigh that might have been classified as a groan. She turned off her ignition, grabbed her bag, and climbed out, resigned to hear whatever Agent Hollywood had for her this time.

"Be careful," she shouted across the roof of her car, making Ian jump. Carlee was more pleased with that than she probably should've been. "The jeweler across the street hates solicitors. She calls the cops on them all the time. And you look like you're trying to sell something."

To his credit, Ian quickly returned to his overly confident, superstar-agent self so fast, Carlee doubted he'd jumped in the first place. He looked at her with a frustratingly perfect smirk. "Are you talking about

Miss Hawthorn?" he asked innocently. "I was just talking to her. She said she liked my tie."

Carlee stopped in front of Ian and gave him a sidelong look, unsure if he was serious or not. Ms. Hawthorn never opened this early on weekends. He was lying to mess with her; he had to be.

"So, what was it you had to tell me in person and not over the phone? And on a Saturday, no less?"

"Saturdays don't mean anything to you," Ian noted—correctly, damn him. "Don't pretend like you wouldn't be working anyway."

Carlee peered at him, trying her hardest to think of a snarky reply. All she came up with was a roll of her eyes as she pushed through the door and started up the stairs, not waiting to see if Ian followed.

"You know me better than to think I'd waste your time, Carlee," Ian insisted without prompting, his voice dropping an octave, as it did when their conversations grew suddenly grave. She focused on the sound of his footsteps tailing her up the stairwell. "You need to hear everything I've found, and I want you to hear it directly from me."

Carlee flipped through her keyring until she found the office key and unlocked the door. Eleanor's desk looked forlorn, empty as it was. A typical Saturday.

She hadn't even pulled the key from the lock when Ian squeezed through behind her, walking into the office first.

"Well, at least I know you're not a vampire," Carlee griped.

Ian squinted at her, genuinely confused. "What on earth are you talking about? Did you smack your head during the last case?"

"Vampires have to be invited in before they can enter homes," Carlee informed him. "Or offices, I guess. And you just walked right in, uninvited."

"You were a big nerd in college, weren't you?" Ian said, but somehow, it sounded remarkably free of judgment. "Anyway, I didn't come here to talk about vampires with you, Carlee. We have more important things to discuss."

"And yet I still don't know what this is about. All you've done is hype up this 'news' that you're so sure I want to hear," Carlee said, closing the door with a showman's push.

She moved to her office, slung her bag down by her desk, and turned to face Ian with crossed arms. His expression—an odd, almost unnerving mixture of unmitigated glee and concern—gave her pause.

"Because it's big," Ian said, approaching the desk. "And you *will* want to hear it."

"Out with it, then," she snapped.

"I know you've been all buddy-buddy with Zack West lately, but what do you know about him? What do you truly know about this partner of yours?"

"Really, Ian?" Carlee asked, exasperated. He nodded. "Okay... He's been a CPD detective for a while, he cares about his family, and he likes home brew. Is that enough for you, or do you want details on his coffee orders too?"

Ian quirked an eyebrow. "Is that it? Aren't you a PI? You've worked with the guy for a month and that's all you've got?"

"Unlike you, Garnett, I don't run covert investigations into my allies."

His smile dropped, and Ian's demeanor became deadly serious. "You should—because Zack's a shitty cop. A *very* shitty cop."

"No, he's not! Why would you say that?"

"Because I ran a background check on him, of course."

Carlee could feel a headache coming on. "Riddle me this: why the hell did you run a background check on my colleague without asking me first?"

"Because you weren't looking into him, and someone had to," Ian said sharply. "You're working elbow to elbow with him and you don't even know what kind of guy he is."

"Honestly, Ian, if that's your breaking news, I think we're done here," she said, waving her hands around to encapsulate the conversation. "I don't care if he's good at his job, okay? All I need is his help."

"You're not taking this seriously, Carlee." Ian squared her up with a stern look. "I'm not telling you this to be a smartass. I'm telling you this to keep you out of harm's way."

"Oh, my, my..." Carlee sat in her chair with a heavy whump. "Aren't you just my knight in shining armor?"

"Zack isn't who you think he is," Ian asserted.

"Sure, Garnett. Whatever you say."

"I mean it."

"Yeah? And so do I. I don't need a chaperone... especially not you."

Ian briefly deflated, then quickly composed himself and launched into his spiel anyway, eager to spill the beans. "I'll tell you what I know, and what you do with it is your own decision, okay? And what I know is that Zack West has made a profession out of cutting corners. Working in the gray."

"I need examples, Ian. I've seen Zack pull some mildly shady maneuvers in the field, but nothing that ever made me think twice about working with him."

"Look deeper, then. The man's jacket is filled to the brim with reprimands and formal disciplinary actions, and those actions have consistently jeopardized convictions. His chronically bad policework puts crooks back on the streets. Does *that* make you think twice?"

"You've worked with the CPD, right?" Carlee asked, unimpressed.

"Yeah. So?"

"Cops run up against yellow tape and sometimes they break it, on accident or on purpose. Sometimes perps get good lawyers and they capitalize on that. Doesn't mean they're *all* bad at their jobs."

"This one is. Whatever comes to mind when you hear 'shitty cop,' Zack West has done it," Ian insisted, growing increasingly irritated.

"Is he dirty?"

"I wish he was, because then there would be an explanation. But he's not and he still has so many write-ups for roughing up suspects and improper handling of evidence, it's basically his modus operandi."

Carlee's eyes narrowed. She wanted to say something, to defend Zack, but she came up short. Ian sensed her hesitance and pounced like a lion closing in for the kill.

"And while I said he wasn't dirty, you should know he's been accused of 'scrubbing' troubling details from his reports," Ian said. "Hell, just a few weeks ago, he nearly sank an investigation by making a move on a suspect before the judge's warrant officially went through."

"I'm sure he has a good enough reason for all of that."

"He'd better since he's habitually on the edge of getting his ass shitcanned."

"It just doesn't add up," Carlee murmured. "The guy gets uncomfortable ordering drinks in a hipster coffee shop. I'm having trouble imagining him roughing up suspects."

"One suspect managed to get a black eye and a bloody nose between his apprehension and the interrogation room. It was written up as a 'trip and fall,' but it's clear as day that West battered the guy. It would've been the third incident in as many months and instigated a formal investigation, so he covered it up."

"What did this guy do?" Carlee asked.

"Does it matter?" Ian returned, glaring at her. "There is a proper way of doing investigative work, and West apparently doesn't give a shit!"

Carlee grunted, her emotions internally running amok. She had known Ian much longer than she had known Zack, and at the end of the day, she trusted his judgment. Annoying or not, she couldn't entirely ignore what he was telling her. She let out a powerful sigh, pinching the bridge of her nose to take her mind off the blooming ache in the back of her head.

She tried to imagine Zack, grumpy and uncomfortable sitting at the Catty Corner, roughing up a suspect and—for the most part—couldn't. But there was a small voice, deep in her subconscious, that murmured *maybe*.

A mirthless laugh escaped her. "CPD's finest, huh?" She shook her head. "Thanks for telling me, Ian. But I'm still going to work with him on this one."

"Does this not worry you?" Ian persisted. "Does it not bother you that he could completely fuck up the Eighth-Grade Killer investigation? That he could cut some corner that ruins everything? What happens when you find them, catch them, and then they go free on a technicality because Zack mishandled the evidence?"

Carlee's breath hitched at the thought. She couldn't even begin to imagine what she would do if that were to happen. Still, she couldn't get tripped up by possible—if improbable—futures. She had a job to do, a killer to catch right there in the present. She shook her head again to clear it.

"Look, I can't afford to be worried about that right now," Carlee said. "We're—I'm—in the middle of the Two-Faced Killer case, and I'm working with him to solve it, whether you think it's a good idea or not. I need his help, his access."

"*I* can be your access, Carlee," Ian insisted, enthusiastically placing his hands on his chest. "I doubt CPD is equipped to handle either of these cases—the Eighth-Grade Killer or the Two-Faced Killer."

"Zack's actually been a great—"

"Zack is just some homicide detective in over his head!" Ian snapped. "And that's going to make him even more likely to cut corners. He doesn't have the experience or the resources that the FBI can bring to bear."

"You mean the experience or resources that *you* can bring to bear," Carlee said, side-eyeing Ian as he slid into the chair across from her. "Please tell me this is something more than interagency jealousy."

"There's nothing jealous about it." A touch of defensiveness tinged his otherwise even-keeled response. She would've missed it had she not known him so well. "I'm merely stating facts."

"You're spreading rumors."

"Am I? Then why don't you tell me what Zack managed to find out about those letters you've been getting?"

The threats. The dark red ink telling Carlee to stay away from her hometown, the sheep hearts in boxes. She had almost forgotten that she'd told Ian about those.

Carlee chewed the inside of her cheek. "Not much," she admitted. "But neither have I."

"That isn't your job," Ian said. "It's his. Have you gotten any new packages?"

"None worth your attention," Carlee mumbled, unwilling to reopen the sheep's heart incident. She could tell he didn't believe her by the quirk of his brow. "Like you said, it's Zack's job to look into them, and that means it's not yours either."

Ian gave her a look like he wanted to press the issue, but after a moment, he shrugged. "If you say so."

They sat in silence as Carlee took in everything Ian said. She was reluctant to rely entirely on anyone, but Ian had been there for her in the past, helping her bypass red tape on investigations, working a case with her when the first threatening letters had arrived, and checking up on her after a knife wound to the neck sent her to the hospital. She could meet him halfway.

"Okay, damn it," she finally relented, though every fiber of her pride squirmed in protest. "You win, all right? I'll bring you in on the Two-Faced Killer investigation... to a point."

Ian didn't fist pump in celebration, nothing so obvious, but Carlee caught the slightest hint of a smirk. It was exactly the touch of smugness she expected from him. "And what, exactly, do you need the Federal Bureau of Investigation to do for you?"

"I'm looking into a Jasmina Callenwood—alias 'Duchess'—a queenpin of the drug trade in Chicago's fashion and beauty industry." Carlee brought up a picture on her computer of a woman at the end of a catwalk, sitting alone, as if the models were there just for her. "I need to talk to her, but I can't figure out how to get in contact."

"Why are you trying to get ahold of a queenpin?"

"Each of the Two-Faced Killer's victims were drugged prior to their murders," Carlee explained, stabbing the picture with her pointer finger as if she could poke through and jab the Duchess herself. "And, if the hushed whispers of the people we've interviewed so far are to be believed, she controls all the drugs in that industry. If the killer is connected, Jasmina is almost certainly involved... or at least knows someone who is."

"And Zack can't get you in?" Ian teased her.

"He can't get a warrant because we don't have any solid evidence," Carlee corrected him. "In as much as a drive-by and cursory search through city records can tell me, it looks like her place is almost as impregnable as mine."

"Impossible," Ian said, leaving out his implied *for you*. "All right, Carlee, I'll look into it."

"Thanks," she said tersely.

Ian chuckled to himself as he stood, indicating she was going to hate the next words out of his mouth. "What would you ever do without me, Carlee Knight?"

"Let's think," she groused, shutting her eyes to disguise the twitch of her left eyelid. "Probably my job. Like I always do."

"Uh-huh," he said playfully. "But maybe a little slower and a little less thoroughly."

Carlee looked at Mocha's controls sitting by her keyboard and wondered how badly he'd be injured if she flew him into Ian's head. Before she could give it a try, though, the door opened and Eleanor stepped in.

"I knew I heard you in here, Carlee," Eleanor said. She nodded at Ian. "And Special Agent Ian Garnett, always a pleasure to run into you."

"You know that the feeling's mutual, Eleanor," he said, holding a hand to his heart. He turned back to Carlee and missed Eleanor's reaction—a scrunched nose like she had stepped in something and smelled it.

"What are you doing here?" Carlee asked.

"I have some documents I need you to look over. But if you're busy..."

"She's not—not anymore. I was actually on my way out. I'll let you know if I turn anything up," Ian said to Carlee before turning to Eleanor, flashing a grin that bordered on greasy. "And it really was a pleasure seeing you, however briefly, Eleanor. Rest assured, my weekend is made."

"As it should be," Eleanor replied, a half-smile on her lips. "Feel free to come back during our normal office hours whenever you need to lift up your day."

Ian made his exit, waving at them as he closed the door. Carlee waited until his footsteps faded down the hall before raising an eyebrow at Eleanor. "Now, cut the bullshit. Coming in on a Saturday? What's wrong?"

"Nothing's wrong, Carlee," Eleanor said playfully. "Why would you think that?"

"Because you said you had documents for me to look at. It sounded urgent."

"Oh, I lied. I don't have any documents. I just figured you needed an excuse to kick Ian out of here." They laughed, but Eleanor's smile quickly faded and she let out an exasperated sigh. "So, now that he's gone, would you mind telling me what the hell you think you're doing?"

"What do you mean?"

"I heard what you two were talking about. A drug dealer? A *queenpin*? Do you have any idea what could happen if you cross someone powerful like that?"

Carlee leaned back in her chair, steepling her fingers. "So you're here to eavesdrop on my conversations, are you? I know what I'm doing."

"Do you?" Eleanor demanded. "Because this is the big leagues, Carlee, and the stakes are much higher than they are with some cheating husband."

"I know that." Maybe it was because of the headache Ian had started, but her spark of annoyance ignited a bonfire instead of a match.

"So let your FBI friend take care of it, then!" Eleanor exclaimed, throwing up her hands. "A drug dealer would hesitate a lot longer to disappear a federal agent than she would a private investigator. You don't have to get involved in these life-and-death investigations. You don't have to put yourself at risk like this!"

"I'm an investigator, Eleanor. This whole job is a risk."

"Exactly! You're an investigator, not a spy," Eleanor said. She didn't plead for anything, but Carlee recognized something adjacent to it in her voice. "Why can't you just leave the dangerous work to the professionals?"

Carlee knew she was just worried about her safety, but she couldn't help but bristle at Eleanor's choice of words. "Am I not also a professional?"

"You know that's not what I meant."

"Look, Eleanor—"

Carlee's phone went off, and *Zack West* appeared on the caller ID. Her finger hesitated over the *answer call* button, but she'd be lying if she said she wasn't grateful for the interruption.

"I need to take this," she said, feeling equal parts relieved and cowardly. Eleanor mouthed *this isn't over* before stepping out of the room. "What is it, Zack?"

"You need to get to the hospital ASAP."

"Now's not the best time," she said, glancing toward the door. "Can you just—"

"Iris's doctor gave me a call."

"Did she... pass?"

"Actually... she's awake."

Chapter Fourteen

Carlee didn't remember Iris's room being so far from the hospital's entrance. She could've sworn it had been right around the corner, but as the nurse in front of her pushed through another set of doors, she realized she had been wrong. The nurse hadn't stopped—talking or walking—since Zack had shown his badge.

"She hasn't spoken yet," the nurse continued, showing no sign of slowing down. "She's responding to stimuli like touch and sound, though."

"That's amazing," Carlee said, remembering the paleness of Iris's skin, the lightness of her breathing, and how tenuous her grip on life had been. "The doctor we talked to seemed pretty convinced she wasn't going to make it."

"None of us expected her to!" the nurse exclaimed. "It's a huge deal!"

"What about the organ failure?" Zack asked.

"She's stable... for now. It's more than any of us could've hoped for, with all that ketamine in her system. It's a miracle she's conscious at all."

The nurse finally stopped outside a door, knocking gently and slowly opening it.

"Miss Livingstone?" she whispered, poking her head through. "Oh, I'm sorry, detectives." The nurse clucked her tongue before she opened the door fully. "It looks like she's sleeping. You can have a seat, but you'll have to wait until she wakes up."

She stepped aside, letting Zack and Carlee into the room. The disappointment of learning Iris had fallen asleep was quickly replaced by the surprise of finding another visitor. An older woman sat in a chair pulled up to the bed, holding Iris's hand in hers.

"Hey, Miss Alford," the nurse said, smiling warmly. "Has Iris been awake at all recently?"

"She's been asleep for a while," Miss Alford said quietly, so as not to disturb Iris. "And I told you to call me Lula, dear."

A smile and a sheepish apology from the nurse, and then she was gone.

Zack and Carlee stood there awkwardly, the rhythmic noises of the machines hooked up to Iris filling the silence.

"Nice to meet you," Zack said to Iris's visitor—Lula.

Carlee gave Lula a close, analytical look. She was a matronly-looking woman with dignified airs, stylish clothing, and perfect makeup. She didn't look like Iris's blood relative, but maybe she'd married into the family. A loving aunt, perhaps?

"Same here," Lula finally said. "I'm so glad to see I'm not the only one concerned about poor Iris. Did I hear the nurse say you two are detectives?"

"Detective Zack West." He jumped in a little too quickly, placing a shockingly polite hand on his chest before motioning toward Carlee. "And this is Carlee Knight, private investigator."

Ian's voice crawled in her head, whispering that Zack wouldn't have been so polite if Lula was a suspect. Carlee struggled not to cringe. She couldn't let him get to her, couldn't let him undermine her working relationship with the man spearheading the official Eighth-Grade Killer case.

"It's a pleasure to meet you, Lula," Carlee said, leaning over to shake Lula's offered hand. She looked over at Iris, still asleep. "While we wait for this one to wake up, would you mind if we chatted with you instead?"

Lula smiled pleasantly. "Of course not. Though I'm not sure how much help I'll be."

"Are you family? I heard Iris's relatives couldn't be here this quickly."

"And they aren't," Lula said, her smile turning rueful. "I'm just an old instructor worried about one of my Aphrodite stars, is all. Her family's flight was delayed, so I volunteered to keep Iris company 'til they get here."

"That's good of you," Zack said. He grabbed a chair from against the wall and brought it close to Iris's bed, sitting down. A soft chuckle escaped his throat. "I had a lot of teachers who would've volunteered to slap me, but I don't know of any who would've sat at my bedside."

See? I told you he has a violent nature, Ian's voice whispered in her head. Carlee clenched her jaw, trying to displace the thought.

"Iris was always special," Lula said, looking down at her. Iris had recovered some color since the last time Carlee had seen her, and her chest rose and fell with much more strength than before. "One of my best, actually."

"Are you two close?" Carlee asked.

"We were quite close at Aphrodite. Such a talented artist. I knew she would go far—everyone knew she would go far. It's such a shame to..." Lula's gaze dropped to the floor as if she knew she'd been about to overstep. "Well, you know. To find her like this."

"Maybe you could help us help her." Carlee motioned to the still-sleeping Iris. "Do you know anyone who might've wanted to hurt her? Any reason someone would want to?"

Lula shook her head, a pained look pinching her face. "She was loved by everyone."

"That's not what I heard," Carlee said, testing the waters. "I understand she was a little confrontational."

"I suppose she was, but all talent is confrontational, isn't it? Still, I can't imagine anyone wanting to actually hurt her."

Carlee and Zack shared a look. They had heard much the same about Janie from Kinzie, but it was growing increasingly clear they would get no closer to the whole truth without talking to Iris herself. Carlee took another chair from the wall and slowly brought it to the bed. She hadn't wanted to give up the psychological upper hand of standing over Lula, but with Zack sitting down, it seemed a useless tactic.

"Has she been awake at all since you've been here?" Zack asked.

Lula shook her head, absentmindedly smoothing a wrinkle out of Iris's blanket. "I'm sure she'll come around any minute now, though."

"Maybe you can tell us a little about yourself while we wait," he said. "What's your story, Lula?"

"Not much of a story—unless you're interested in makeup and fashion." She gave Zack a look that said she doubted he was.

"You'd be surprised." It was a lie—Zack was firing up a subtle interrogation—but given what Carlee knew about his overwhelming lack of subtlety, like a burglar who used a sledgehammer rather than a lockpick, it seemed like a good idea to steer this conversation herself.

"I think my colleague is, in his own way, struggling to make pleasant conversation," Carlee said, rolling her eyes theatrically. Zack glanced at her with a mix of annoyance and gratitude. "You mentioned Aphrodite. Do you still teach there?"

"No, not so much these days. I'm happily retired, though I've been teaching master classes at Aphrodite on and off for years." That did it. At one mention of her professorial history, Lula's modesty was betrayed by the eagerness in her voice. Typical teacher.

"That sounds satisfying," Carlee lied.

"More than anything else, I'm just an old hand trying to step back for the new generation, helping where I can."

"How's retirement been treating you?" Zack asked, regaining his footing now that Carlee had the ball rolling. "Are you past the stir-crazy period?"

"Oh, I skipped that phase entirely," Lula said, chuckling to herself.

"Why?" he asked.

"It felt right, and you know what? It *was* right. It was a relief. I couldn't keep up with the insane hours that models and artists work anymore."

"Could you keep up with that before Aphrodite?" Carlee pushed.

"When I was younger, I relished the insanity. A couple decades ago, at the height of my career, I suppose you could say I was near the top of the field itself?" Lula's voice lilted up to make it a question, but it was clear that she was still trying to be modest.

"Were you working on something I might know?"

"You wouldn't know any of the campaigns—makeup artists rarely become household names." Her hand went from Iris's bed to her chest. "But I worked for some of the bigs. The Sienna photoshoot, the Black Chute commercials... to name a couple."

"Wait, the Sienna photoshoot?" Zack asked, trying but failing to keep his voice from betraying his bewilderment. "You mean that one with the flowy hospital gown in the desert? You worked on that?"

"Flowy hospital gown?" Carlee turned to him, wide-eyed. "Really?"

He shrugged. "I had the poster on my wall in college. Sue me."

Lula laughed, delighted that her work had been recognized. "That shoot was awful. Sand everywhere. I was pouring it out of my shoes months later."

"Well, I think I speak for a lot of boys when I say, 'Thank you for your service,' Lula," Zack said, laughing at the nostalgia of his pervy underclassman years. Carlee shot him her best "gross" look, but it didn't seem to faze him.

"You're not the first man to tell me that, Detective West," Lula said, her smile turning wry. "Believe it or not, it took me quite a while to break in. A lot of models back then didn't want some snot-nosed youngster doing their makeup, but that shoot opened doors for me, and from then on, it all just sort of clicked into place."

Lula sat back, basking in the glow of her glory years, not caring if it didn't mean anything to Carlee.

Bamboozled by how quickly their interview had flipped in Zack's favor, Carlee mentally scrambled for another question to keep Lula going. "So, how plugged into the industry are you these days? Because I've been trying to get my hands on some Facade by Jaq Curwood for a while now and haven't had any luck. Any chance you could help me out with that?"

Zack raised his eyebrow at her for the ham-fisted segue, and Carlee inwardly winced. It seemed he wasn't the only one capable of bulling their way through a china shop.

"I'm afraid that makes two of us, Miss Knight," Lula confessed, chasing her words with a sigh. "You should know it's all just a gimmick. I've gotten ahold of Jaq Curwood products a couple of times, and honestly? You can find better at department stores."

Carlee was sure Lula was about to dive into a mini-lecture on makeup products when, suddenly, Iris's leg twitched in the hospital bed, and all three of them shot up around her. After a few moments of bated breath, her eyelids fluttered, as if coming out of a long sleep.

"Iris!" Lula grasped her hand and leaned in toward her. "Iris, sweetheart, can you hear me?"

"What's... um..." Iris blinked deerishly, her eyes slowly focusing before going wide as they centered in on Lula.

"Easy, now... it's okay," Lula soothed, stroking Iris's forearm as the girl's breathing grew sharp and her gaze darted fearfully from the machines to the sterile white walls. "You're in the hospital, but you're doing so much better, and everything will be all right."

"You're safe, Iris," Zack added helpfully. "I'm Detective Zack West with the Chicago Police Department, and this is Carlee Knight, a private investigator. We're here to help you get through this."

"We're going to find out who put you in this position, Iris," Carlee said. "And we're going to bring them to justice. Don't you worry."

Iris's eyes shimmered at Carlee and she opened her mouth as if to speak, but nothing came out. She tried again with the same result and frowned, then looked from Carlee to Lula, like she wanted her mentor to translate for her. Swallowing hard, she started to shiver with what looked like the onset of tears.

"Your family's on the way, dear," Lula said, laying her hand on Iris's shoulder. "They'll be here soon."

"You'll..." Iris coughed.

Lula didn't need her to finish the sentence. "Yes, dear. I will. I'll be right here with you until they walk through that door. I'm not going anywhere."

Iris's wide eyes shifted from Lula to Zack to Carlee and back to Lula before she nodded, her rapid breathing finally slowing down.

"I hate to have to ask this right when you wake up," Zack said, brows furrowing, looking genuinely stricken, "but do you remember anything?"

His questions spilled out of him like a tidal wave, crashing against the still-fragile Iris as if she were an unsuspecting and unprepared swimmer. When was she attacked, how did she get away, where was she—all important questions that Carlee was desperate to know the answers to, but all useless in Iris's current state. Zack had come in too hard and too fast and only managed to overwhelm Iris completely.

An image of Ian Garnett sat in the back of Carlee's mind, his arms crossed, eyebrows raised. *Told you so*, he said. Carlee forced him out.

"Detective," Iris choked, her voice raspy from disuse.

"You can call me Zack. Zack and Carlee," he added, making a surge of something distasteful hit the back of Carlee's throat. Suddenly, she didn't like how easily he jammed their names together.

"Zack. And Carlee," Iris echoed, looking back and forth between them. Carlee nodded at her. "I'm really sorry, but…" Her voice hitched, and Lula leaned in closer, patting her hand.

"It's okay, Iris, take your time."

"I just…" Tears welled in Iris's eyes as she looked at Lula, who squeezed her fingers as if to give her the strength to continue.

"Don't be alarmed, dear. We all just want to know what happened. That's it," Lula reassured her.

"I guess I… I think I don't remember anything."

"Nothing?" Lula's voice broke. "You don't remember taking drugs or walking around the park?" She gave Iris's hand another squeeze.

"Um… No. The last thing I remember is walking into the corner store," Iris managed before she burst into dry sobs, the reality of her circumstances crashing down on her.

Lula rubbed her shoulder and cooed *there, there*, like a doting mother.

"I'm so sorry," Iris wept, and the EKG began to beep faster.

"You didn't do anything wrong, Iris," Zack said. "You don't need to apologize."

"Of course you don't," Carlee added, her heart clouding over at the distress she and Zack had put Iris through. "It's going to be okay, Iris. I promise it will be."

The door opened, and the nurse who led them to the room poked her head back in. She took one look at the distraught expression on Iris's face and immediately started bustling Carlee, Zack, and Lula out. "Feel free to wait in the lobby, and I'll come back and grab you once I've checked her over," she insisted, leaving no room for argument.

"I'm not going far, honey," Lula promised, giving Iris one last pat on the hand. "Just remember, I'm right outside your door."

Iris nodded bravely, even while a tear rolled down her face.

The three of them found their way back to the lobby, where they resettled in a corner stuffed with plump leather chairs.

"I'm glad you're here, Lula," Carlee said, uneasy with the silence that had fallen over them. "You're really, really good with her."

Zack nodded his agreement. "Thanks for calming her down. It made everything easier—on Iris and on us too."

Lula shook her head, folding her hands in her lap. "There's no need to thank me. I love all my students, and as I said, Iris is special."

"I'm sure she's grateful to have you by her side. And after the career you had, I'd bet it's a lot easier to deal with students than models," Zack slipped in. Carlee almost whacked him for his half-assed attempt to lighten the mood, but in another victory for Camp West, Lula chuckled.

"Don't get me wrong, there is *plenty* of gossip and politics at Aphrodite," she said. "But even the worst of it was better than the lightest stuff I dealt with day-to-day in the industry. After experiencing how cutthroat shoots and catwalks are, it was easy for me to keep above all of that."

"You said before that you didn't care for the Jaq Curwood stuff you'd used," Carlee said, trying her best to play off her bluntness as the natural flow of conversation. "Since you obviously know the brand, I wonder... do you know Jasmina Callenwood?"

Lula chortled as if Carlee had asked something incredibly foolish. "I've been on the scene for decades now, dear. Of course I know Jasmina Callenwood. You can hardly throw a rock at a show and not hit some old veteran of the industry who's beholden to Jasmina... or has a vendetta against her. And you didn't hear it from me, but I've been told she's been dabbling in more than just makeup." Lula narrowed her eyes but let her words die off.

"Do you know her personally?" Carlee probed, picking up on Lula's not-so-subtle hints and giving her an excuse to continue.

"I was out of the game by the time she really started to make a name for herself." Lula tilted her head back and forth before throwing her hands up. "But yes, I've worked with the Duchess."

The Duchess.

There it was, right out of the mouth of an industry expert: Jaq Curwood was Jasmina Callenwood. And Jasmina Callenwood was, indeed, the Duchess. The queenpin, the one who could have given Janie her makeup and—quite possibly—her ketamine.

Zack laughed softly next to Carlee; the noise made her wince. "You makeup people can't honestly call her that, right?"

"Us makeup people?" Lula shot Zack a withering gaze that made him fold into himself a fraction. Enough, at least, that Carlee didn't have to elbow him in his ribs.

"I'm sure this is a long shot, but... you don't still know how to get ahold of her, do you?" Carlee asked, trying not to get her hopes up.

"You think she had something to do with what happened to Iris?" The idea seemed to distress Lula. "I hope not, because Jasmina is..." She trailed off, suddenly reluctant to gossip.

"From what I can tell, she's a ghost unless you have the right connections," Carlee said.

Lula's demeanor changed in front of Carlee's eyes, the matronly teacher turning into a ruthless, calculating professional. Carlee was certain that she'd been a force to be reckoned with back in her heyday. "Maybe it's best to leave ghosts where they lie?"

"Thanks for the heads up, but I really need to talk to this particular ghost. Could you help us get in touch with her?"

"I guess, but are you *sure* that's what you want?" Lula asked seriously. "The Duchess is not someone to trifle with. And I mean that in every single sense of the word."

"Is that a threat?" Carlee asked, equally as serious.

"It's a warning," Lula said. "One you'll need, I'm afraid."

"Because...?"

"Because I can do better than just putting you in touch with her. I can arrange a meeting, but you should know that if you want an audience with the Duchess, you'd better be prepared for all her glory."

Chapter Fifteen

I pushed the box, heavy as it was, along the hallway. The furniture dolly helped, but at the end of the day, it was still slick plastic wheels on surprisingly thick carpet. I would have to leave a scathing review about this on the furniture store's website.

I chuckled to myself. The mundanity of it all struck me as particularly comedic, all things considered. I had passed a couple of tenants by now, and not a single one suspected what was in the box. Not a single one had offered to help me, either, but I supposed I couldn't complain too much about that. Mundanity was the whole purpose of my disguise after all.

Wear a simple, blue-collar jumpsuit—in this case, a moving company uniform, complete with a name tag—and you might as well not exist to the yuppie class. I briefly wondered if anyone could even recall passing me in the hall. Later, when my labors bore fruit, they would desperately try to remember any particular detail about me, but I knew they wouldn't. If anything, they would make up details. Craft some story about an obviously evil being, or wonder aloud why they hadn't acted when they passed me.

It was always the same story. If their testimonies ever made it into the newspaper, they would do nothing but give me a laugh. Their desperation to be helpful would only work in my favor as they turned me into some hulking, seven-foot-tall menace. No one ever remembered specifics, even when they knew they should.

I looked myself over one more time and admired the simplicity of the plan, the butter-smooth execution. Simplicity had also opened up the door to my target.

People should really know better than to answer every innocent ring of their bell. But that was their undoing, not mine.

My target had been hesitant about opening the door. It had taken a little smooth talking on my part—a delivery and an appliance installation, and I would be gone. In and out.

It had done the trick. She'd let me in. She had been alone, like I knew she would be.

"Hold the door," I called to a man in the elevator. I pushed the box in and maneuvered it into the corner. "First floor, please."

My temporary companion didn't even give the box a second look as he pressed the button, and we started to descend.

"Got you working on a Saturday, huh?" he asked, not as comfortable with the quiet as I was.

"You know it." I made a little huff of discontentment. "Evil bastards."

That garnered a laugh of commiseration as the elevator finally settled on the first floor, and the doors opened. I pushed my quarry out, but the wheels started to slip on the carpet.

My companion gave a gruff sigh but helped me push all the same. "Thanks, pal," I said.

When we finally managed to get the box rolling, he rushed to hold the back door of the condominium open for me and wished me a good day. Of course, I smiled and wished him a good day right back. But he didn't see my smile, for he had already turned around to trot up the long hallway and toward the garage.

Moments later, I was out in the warm, open air, my lungs grateful for the change of humidity. The dolly squeaked to a halt beside the car—not my own, of course—that was waiting patiently for me.

I fished the keys out of my pocket and opened the trunk without incident. It was a cruel irony that, given my diminished physical state, this next task would be the most challenging part of the entire plan.

It took a great deal of effort to lift the box, even that small distance. Carlee's face in my mind's eye drove me as my arms quivered, as my legs threatened to buckle, but the question I so wanted to ask her wouldn't allow me to quit. Later, I would have to thank her for the motivation.

At one point, the contents of my box shuffled, and my heart stilled. But the noise stopped, and I heaved it into the trunk, huffing and puffing.

I wiped the sweat from my brow and drank in the sight. There it was, my prize, sitting perfectly in its automobile sepulchre.

My hand quivered ever so slightly as I reached for the top, and it was only with great discipline that I didn't rip the box open to behold its contents. Instead, I grabbed my pocketknife, stabbed it into the side, and wiggled it around until the hole was big enough to let air in.

The hole was also big enough for me to peer inside.

"Shh," I hissed as I stroked her curly black hair, nestled around her pretty little face.

Still asleep. All according to plan.

Chapter Sixteen

Carlee had met countless body language experts. She vividly remembered a college criminology class in which the guest speaker—a bona fide FBI profiler—had called her classmates up and read them like a book in front of everyone.

She knew she was a far cry from an FBI-certified body language authority, but as she watched Zack adjust his tie for the umpteenth time, Carlee couldn't help but notice he seemed just a *little* uncomfortable.

"What's going on with you today?" she asked, raising an eyebrow.

He flattened his hand over the tie. "Nothing."

From her uncomfortable seat in the FBI office lobby, Carlee reclined on the bench and tried to figure out how they'd transported a large, live white oak inside the atrium. No matter how many times she found herself waiting in this very building, she'd never quite figured it out.

"The glass wall must pop out, don't you think?" she asked, tilting her head. There didn't appear to be any obvious way for the whole facade of the atrium to move, but maybe she'd missed it. "Do you think they built around it? How old do you think that tree is, anyway?"

"What the hell are you talking about?" Zack side-eyed her like she'd grown a second head. They had been sitting there for ten minutes, and he clearly hadn't registered a word she'd said.

She scoffed, but Zack's attention drifted off again before she could say anything. He distractedly flipped his visitor's badge between his fingers.

She'd brought Zack there to confer with Ian so the three of them could put their heads together and figure out the best way to approach Duchess Callenwood. Three heads were usually better than two, but looking at Zack now—his face closed off, his arms crossed—made her doubt the old adage.

"Hey," she said, grabbing Zack's shoulder. He jumped, if only a nanometer, but settled quickly. "You don't need to be nervous. Ian's good. He can help us."

"I'm sure he is," he said, grunting as if the admission physically pained him. "But I still don't think we need to rope the FBI into this."

"We're not. We're roping *Ian* into this. He's helped me out with many cases in the past, so I know he's sharp, and he won't officially bring the Bureau in unless he has to. Unless I ask him to. I trust him."

Zack grunted again with less vigor. "I guess that makes one of us..."

Did he seem reluctant to work with people who had more authority than him, or was Ian's voice worming inside her head? If it was, it was unfair, since his actual voice would be worming around in her ear soon enough. Not for the first time, Carlee wondered whether she should thank Ian for his nosiness or punch him.

"Plus," she added, leaning in and lowering her voice to a conspiratorial whisper, "if we're going to pull off a sting, we'll need to work with an expert, and Ian's just that."

Zack's eyes rolled when she used the term "expert," but otherwise, she appreciated that he didn't further his protests.

Soon after, she heard the familiar clicks of Ian's leather shoes coming down the hall. He crossed into the atrium and found her in an instant. His beaming smile tempered only when he recognized Zack sitting next to her.

Suddenly, intense doubt about introducing these two crept into Carlee's mind. She tried to smile as brightly as she could, intercepting Ian and reaching out to shake his hand.

"Thanks for doing this," she said, motioning between him and Zack to facilitate introductions.

Ian tilted his head at her as if he thought her formality was somehow cute. "Anything for you, Carlee."

"This is CPD Detective Zack West. And Zack, this is Special Agent Ian Garnett."

"Pleasure," Zack said through a strained smile, shaking Ian's hand.

"Your reputation precedes you, Detective West," Ian said. If a smile could slap someone across the face, Ian's would have. Zack shot Carlee a not-so-subtle glare. "Always a pleasure to meet with Chicago's finest."

The two men stood there as if frozen in time, shaking hands in what Carlee could tell was a death grip, a boneheaded test of each other's manliness. They stood there so long, Carlee started to worry that she had accidentally let slip to Zack that Ian had looked into his service record, but she knew she hadn't.

"Well, now that we've all met..." Carlee clapped once, loudly, trying to knock both off-kilter enough that they might let go. "Why don't we get down to business?"

Their hands dropped simultaneously, as if they had reached some psychic agreement that Carlee wasn't privy to. She breathed a sigh of relief that their stupid handshake hadn't devolved into some caveman dominance contest.

Morons, Carlee mouthed to herself when they weren't looking, trying to keep her supreme annoyance off her face. These two men confounded her on an average day. This, however, was an exceptional level of convoluted behavior.

"Since the CPD is here," Ian went on, his smile convincing Carlee it had been engineered to annoy Zack as efficiently as possible, "I took the initiative to reserve a room."

"That's very gracious of you," Zack said sarcastically. "Lead the way."

"Follow me." Ignoring the tension even as he obviously relished it, Ian led them into a sweeping conference room. Carlee's gaze raced about, cataloging the amenities: a large screen against the back wall with a long, heavy oak table running down the length of it, and plush leather chairs that each must've cost as much as all the furniture in her office waiting room. If Ian wanted to rub Zack's nose in the FBI's grandiosity, he was succeeding.

Zack plopped himself in a seat at the table, turning to Carlee and Ian as if he was tired of wasting time. She took up a chair across from him, and with a shrug of his shoulders, Ian filled the chair at the end.

"Okay, it's brass tacks time," Carlee said, cutting off both Zack and Ian before they could get into another pissing match. "Let's put our heads together to see how I am going to handle this meeting with the Duchess."

"Is that really happening?" Ian asked, leaning forward in his chair, far too keen.

"I told you that's what I need your help with."

"Yeah, but I thought that was just wishful thinking. Since when do you have a meeting set with the Duchess?"

"A contact we made in the industry offered to set Carlee up with a face-to-face," Zack answered, clearly pleased he knew something Ian didn't. "As long as she goes in with a false name and doesn't give up our investigation, it'll be okay."

"Exactly. And unfortunately for us, the Duchess is not your typical dealer," Carlee said, pulling up the brief she'd written on the wall-mounted screen. A blurry picture of Jasmina, taken by a paparazzo in downtown Chicago during a fashion show, filled the frame. "We needed an introduction because she doesn't accept random appointments, so..."

"So we made that happen," Zack interrupted, earning a hard look from Carlee.

"Though that was only step one," she said. "Jasmina Callenwood accepts invitees on her turf, meeting each one-on-one in her home."

Ian rubbed his chin. "But does it have to be you?"

Was Carlee imagining things, or was that a touch of genuine concern in his voice?

"It does," she answered. "The Duchess only caters to women, so... sorry, boys. That means I'll be going solo."

Zack grunted. "Like hell it does. Under no circumstances are you going to meet with her on your own."

"Excuse me?" Carlee grunted right back, her brows hiking up. Zack had been sullen and surly since they'd walked into the building, but if he was going to turn loose on anyone, she'd expected it to be Ian—not her. "It has to be me," she stressed. "Or which one of you manly men is going undercover as a fashionista?"

Zack shook his head, digging his heels in. "Absolutely not, Carlee. We'll think of another way. I'm not about to let a civilian put herself at risk like that."

"Carlee is hardly a run-of-the-mill civilian," Ian pointed out.

"I don't care," Zack said, fixing Ian with a hard stare, before turning his stern, immovable-object gaze to Carlee. "It's too dangerous to send you in there by yourself. If you're going in, I'm going in with you, and that's that."

"Okay, and how am I supposed to explain the giant man tailing me to Jasmina? 'Hi, I'm here for my very exclusive one-on-one with a powerful drug dealer. Do you mind that I brought my super normal, totally unsuspicious friend?'"

Zack huffed. "Then I'll go as your bodyguard. She handles the rich and famous, doesn't she? It won't be strange if you show up with protection."

"No dice, Zack," Carlee said. "Lula said she meets with clients individually. I doubt she'll talk to me if I show up with some goon hovering over my shoulder."

"I agree with Carlee," Ian said, earning himself a grateful glance from her and a less-than-grateful glare from Zack. For the briefest of moments, Carlee didn't automatically want to slap the grin off his irritatingly handsome face. "There's no point in jeopardizing the operation—or your investigation, by the way—by trying to bend Callenwood's rules."

"And what would you know about this investigation?" Zack asked, his voice barely containing the challenge.

Ian's lips pressed into a tight smile. "Plenty, actually." He turned to Carlee, deliberately cutting Zack out. "You'll have to go in by yourself, but you won't be alone, per se. You'll wear a wire... one of ours. The FBI has trailblazing tech, impossible to detect by some midlevel dealer like the Duchess."

"Thank you, Agent Garnett," Carlee said, using Ian's title as a sword against Zack's stubborn shield. She hoped Ian didn't take her approval and run. Giving him something to be even smugger about was almost as bad as Zack's doubt.

"And then what?" Zack was almost baring his teeth. "Are you going to take responsibility if something goes wrong?"

"I will, but I'm curious to know, Detective West—why do you seem so sure Carlee will screw this up?" Ian asked, cloyingly innocent.

"That's not what I said," Zack ground out, absolutely simmering. "Things *might* go wrong. Call me crazy, but I think we need to acknowledge how intensely shit could hit the fan if we send an inexperienced mole into a lion's den."

Ian didn't call him crazy, but he did shrug and say, "Well, I trust her," which Zack took about as well. "In fact, I think she's the only one who can pull this operation off."

A swell of vindication washed through Carlee—and she kind of hated that.

"I'm *right* here, Zack," she said, shooting him a scowl. "And I've done plenty of undercover work before. I'm not some rookie, you know?"

"You haven't done undercover work like *this*, Carlee, and you know it, or you wouldn't have come here, asking an expert for help," Zack insisted.

She fumed at the disrespect, but it was true. Her usual undercover work of tailing cheating husbands to massage parlors couldn't hold a candle to a tête-à-tête with a drug queenpin.

"There's a first time for everything," Ian countered smoothly. "And we won't be far. While we're on the subject, how much undercover work have *you* done on this level, Detective?"

And there it was, Ian's ulterior motive. He was goading Zack, trying to provoke him in front of Carlee to prove his point about Zack's problematic history with the CPD. The joke was on him, though: it only made her more annoyed with both of them.

Judging from the purple shade of Zack's face, he looked like he was moments from launching into Ian when Carlee's phone went off on the table. Their collective attention fell upon the screen like it had just screamed.

Unknown Caller.

Carlee gulped. Steeling herself, she slid the answer bar and put it on speaker.

"Is this Georgia Smith?" the feminine, imperious voice on the other end began, every syllable bouncing off the walls of the almost-empty conference room. It was a voice that demanded answers.

"This is she," Carlee replied with all the confidence she could muster, recognizing the alias Lula had given her. She swooped her voice up high, realizing a moment too late that it wasn't necessary to do an *impression* of a woman in her twenties.

"Lovely," the caller said, crisp and efficient, not inviting conversation. "This is Jasmina. A good friend of mine let me know you'd be interested in sampling my product."

Stopped only by the table, Zack and Ian crowded around, each trying to motion their instructions to her—Zack's "slow down" competing against Ian's "hurry up."

"That's right," Carlee said, holding up a hand to get them to stop. She tried to put some stoicism into her voice, but she could feel a little trill edge into her words. "I hear you only serve the best."

"'Best' doesn't do it justice, dear," Jasmina said, somehow warm and inviting while also cool and regal. "But you'll see for yourself soon enough."

"Sooner rather than later, I hope. When could I meet with you?" Carlee asked, her heart starting to beat faster. This meeting could break the investigation wide open and bring down the Two-Faced Killer once and for all. She had to give herself time to prepare, to make sure she was absolutely ready. "I was thinking Friday?"

Four days to perfect her Georgia Smith persona. She would need every minute between now and then to ensure she could pull it off. The stakes couldn't have been higher.

"Didn't you just say you wanted to meet ASAP?" Jasmina asked.

Carlee heard her smile, a smile that rivaled that of the planet's apex predators—a baring of teeth just as vicious as any tiger or shark. The hairs on the back of her neck stood on end.

"I have a busy week ahead."

"Well..." Jasmina let the pause thicken. Then, with that same smile in her voice, she closed the trap. "If you want the best, you *will* find the time to meet with me tomorrow."

Chapter Seventeen

The wrought iron gate towered above Carlee, an intimidating but beautifully sculpted reminder that the house beyond was, in Lula's own words, not something to be trifled with.

The dozens of cameras Carlee had spotted were anachronistic atop the medieval stone privacy fence surrounding the property. Still, she did not doubt for a moment how effective they were. She knew that camera well—it was the exact same model she used at Castle Carlee.

Castle Carlee. It might be time to think of a different name, Carlee thought. Standing face-to-face with an actual, honest-to-god castle perched near the lakeshore made her condo look more like a tenement than any place befitting royalty. Calling it a castle felt like a joke she wasn't in on.

She pressed the doorbell button next to the gate, desperately trying not to totter in her expensive shoes and faceplant into the sidewalk. Other than a curt buzz, there was no indication it had done anything. The gate didn't unlock, and there was no obvious intercom system to request an audience.

"Did I have to wear heels?" Carlee whispered, doing her best not to move her lips in front of the camera pointed directly at her. "Eleanor's going to kill me if I snap one of them."

"You're supposed to be the new fashion industry hotness, Carlee," Ian piped into her discreet earpiece. He and Zack were a block away in an unmarked van, listening to everything via the wire she had concealed under her blouse. "You can't just walk up wearing sneakers."

"Are you saying I couldn't pull that off?" Carlee hissed. She might be sartorially challenged, but she was fairly sure she knew more about women's fashion than Ian Garnett. "I could be making a statement. Sneakers could be avant-garde, and I could be on the cutting edge."

"Are they, though?" Zack chimed in, asking sincerely.

"Yeah, Carlee. Are they?" Ian joined in, less sincerely.

She subtly flicked at her shirt, thumping the mic concealed beneath. She had to suppress a smile as she heard Ian shout on the other end, recoiling from the audio feedback she had just sent straight to their headsets.

"Damn it, Carlee. It was a joke!"

"And I had no part in it, yet here I am, going deaf," Zack added.

She could imagine both of them sweating in the hot van, holding the headphones away from their ears in pain. If she had to suffer in heels, at least they had to suffer too.

She began to fidget, pulling at the sleeves of the nice silk blouse, making sure they were in their proper places against her wrists. Eleanor had walked her through how everything should look as she wore it, and she mentally went down the checklist while she waited for the gate to open.

When she asked Eleanor to borrow an outfit that would help her pose as a member of the local elite, Carlee had neglected to mention the "wealthy person of interest" she was about to interview was also quite possibly a notorious drug dealer. But no matter how much she did or did not tell her, Eleanor—of course—had been perceptive enough to see at least halfway through Carlee's bullshit.

"Remember, use the phrase 'my husband is calling me' if you have to bail," Ian instructed her via the earpiece, dragging her back to the present.

"We're only a block away," Zack said. "We can be there in five minutes. Tops."

As Carlee tried her hardest to stay calm and not sweat through Eleanor's blouse under the hot July sun, the front door to the stately house finally opened, and an older woman in a traditional maid's outfit came toward her.

"Georgia Smith, I presume," the woman said. Carlee nodded as she pulled the gate open. "Please, if you'll follow me. My mistress is waiting."

"Mistress?" Zack wheezed through the earpiece. "Jesus Christ, this is turning into a bad blue movie."

Carlee discreetly coughed and flicked the mic again, earning her another round of groans.

She carefully picked her way up the limestone steps in her precarious footwear. At the top, the maid pulled the tall, mahogany door open and stepped aside, motioning for Carlee to enter.

Her heels clicked on the ebony and ivory-checked tile of the entrance hallway, and Carlee was forced to take a moment to catch her breath. She had stepped into a sprawling, ornately decorated lobby, something that felt like it had been ripped from the pages of the Roaring Twenties novels she had to read about in high school.

"Please," the maid said, bustling past her. "We mustn't keep the mistress waiting."

She led Carlee to another pair of large double doors that revealed a marvelous sitting room, confirming above all else that Carlee had never set foot in a house anything like the one she found herself in now.

Wood-paneled walls with wide, expansive windows surrounded several thick, lush rugs lying over wood flooring, and velvet couches sitting atop carved, clawed feet. Everything in the room, however, seemed to tilt toward the single, highbacked chair—more like a throne—at its center. And in that chair perched the Duchess, Jasmina Callenwood.

The long, high-necked, purple satin jacket she wore might as well have been a royal mantle, the way it sat on her shoulders over an impossibly crisp white shirt, decorated with several intricate gold necklaces. Her legs were crossed as if she were constantly being made to wait and wasn't happy about it. Jasmina's perfectly painted nails tapped rhythmically against the carved wooden armrest.

"Your guest, Duchess," the maid said. "Miss Georgia Smith."

Jasmina didn't respond, only nodded her dismissal. The maid actually curtseyed before she shuffled away, off to complete whatever chore was next on her list.

Without the maid, the room took on an even more imperious air, which was further facilitated by Jasmina's critical look. She made no move to stand and greet Carlee, not even to speak. She just looked and judged.

"Miss Callenwood, I just—" Carlee started lamely before Jasmina raised two fingers, cutting her off midsentence.

"You will refer to me as 'Duchess,'" she said, her voice somehow airy and steel-backed all at once. "Is that clear?"

"Yes," Carlee said. She then quickly added, "Duchess."

"Good," Jasmina said. "Here in Chicago, I am royalty, and this is my court. You will treat it as such. Are we clear?"

"Of course, Duchess," Carlee said, bowing her head.

"Is this lady for real?" Zack asked in her ear. "No wonder the CNET guys don't want to bother with her."

"The CNET guys don't know enough to know they *should* be bothering with her," Ian responded, annoyed.

Jasmina then held out a limp hand in front of her. Carlee moved to shake it before the Duchess pulled it back, a look of disgust flashing across her face.

Both Lula and Kinzie had warned Carlee that Jasmina could be lightly described as esoteric, and it took a moment for the cue to make sense to her. Carlee suppressed a grimace as she lifted Jasmina's hand, kissing her large sapphire ring. She looked up to see Jasmina smiling and breathed a sigh of relief.

"You may sit," Jasmina said, waving her hand toward a much less stately chair to her left. An empty coffee table sat between them.

"May I say something about that?" Carlee nodded at the door the maid had retreated through, and went on only after receiving silent approval from the Duchess. "An actual maid's outfit? A little overboard, don't you think?"

"Not at all," Jasmina said, more playful than annoyed. "What we wear should tell people who we are, what we do. Kind of like a uniform. You knew exactly who she is the moment you saw her. You knew exactly who I am the moment you saw me."

Jasmina flourished her hands around her. In the outfit, Carlee had to admit she was right—there was no mistaking her for anything but new-world royalty.

"And I know exactly who *you* are," she told Carlee, "just by looking at you."

"And who do you think I am, if you don't mind my asking, Duchess?"

"You are..." Jasmina gave her words a suitable amount of pomp. "Traditional." She smiled wickedly as if she had torn Carlee in half with only three words.

Carlee was reasonably sure that Eleanor would've slapped the shit out of Jasmina if she'd heard that insult about her clothes. But she merely sat down, nodding her deference, wondering what the hell she'd gotten herself into this time.

"I've granted you permission to enter my court today off the word of Lula Alford," Jasmina said, cocking her head. "She might be past her prime, but I can't deny her contribution to the industry. You, however, are an unknown. So why has Lula decided to take you under her wing, I wonder?"

"Lula recognizes rising talent," Carlee said. "I consider myself lucky."

"I'm not so sure you should," Jasmina countered, her voice oozing with pomposity.

"Why is that?"

"Because you might have hitched your wagon to a falling star."

"Lula?"

"Yes. She still commands some respect, hence my agreement to this meeting, but it's fading fast."

"That's why I wanted to see you, Duchess," Carlee said, pivoting quickly to Jasmina's challenge. "I've been told you have access to the best, and I'll need it if I want to achieve everything I plan to achieve here in Chicago."

"You've been told the truth." Jasmina looked Carlee over with an appraising eye, the corner of her mouth curling ever so slightly. "And your timing is lucky. I just got back from Milan. Had you asked last week, I wouldn't have been able to see you."

Carlee had been preparing for this portion of the meeting ever since she had received Jasmina's call, researching as much as she possibly could about the fashion and beauty industry. The sheer amount of it—the brands, the tradeshows, the history of it all—had overwhelmed her, but she had covered as much ground as she possibly could.

"I knew you were in Milan," Carlee said smoothly. "That's the reason I waited to ask for the introduction."

"Have you been to Milan?"

Carlee nodded, starting with the truth. "Once, a few years back. Adored the show, hated the city." She finished with a lie—she'd been there on a case.

"Oh, really?" Jasmina asked, honestly surprised. "Why, might I ask?"

"Yeah, why?" Ian asked in her ear. "I love Milan. It's a wonderful city, beautiful architecture, fabulous museums—"

"It was a little too dirty for my tastes," Carlee said, cutting ear-Ian off. "I much preferred Paris."

"Ah, Paris," Jasmina said, her eyes lighting up. "I take it you've been to the Elysian Tradeshow, then?"

Carlee quickly ran through the shows she had researched but came up empty. She simply hadn't had the time to go over them all. "Not yet, unfortunately," she said, deciding to keep it vague. "But I'm hoping to go soon, once I've made a name for myself here."

"Of course." Jasmina's smile spread, and Carlee breathed another sigh of relief. "You keep talking about making a name for yourself here. Did you make a name for yourself elsewhere? I guess you must have since you managed to catch the eye of the once mighty Lula Alford."

"I was mostly working in Southeast Asia," Carlee said. She'd read it was a rising star in the fashion world, new and raw among the more established circles, meaning she could make some pretty big claims and rest assured that Jasmina wouldn't know every show or model intimately.

"Tidak, kamu tidak, jalang," Jasmina said, switching effortlessly to a foreign language, her eyes sparkling.

If Carlee had been drinking water, she would've spit it all out. As it was, she coughed on dry air. "You'll have to excuse me. I don't understand the language."

"I spent some time in Singapore myself," Jasmina explained. "I assume that's where you were?"

"Pull it together, Carlee," one of the boys breathed in her ear, though she couldn't tell which one. It didn't exactly settle her nerves. "Tell her you were in—"

"Shanghai, actually," Carlee managed to say, her mind racing to cover her lie. "I found the Chinese market to be a blank canvas for me to work on."

"Oh, it's definitely an underserved market," Jasmina said. "I'll have to look up your work later."

"Please do," Carlee said quickly. She needed to get the Duchess on track and off her backstory. "Though I hate to take up so much of your valuable time, Duchess. I was told you were the person to come to when someone needed certain *tools of the trade* to get ahead?"

Carlee used the phrase Lula told her would signal to Jasmina she was a hopeful buyer ready to look at her high-end drugs. She saw a spark of understanding in the Duchess's eyes.

"But of course." Jasmina's smile took a wicked turn. She reached for a sterling silver bell that rested on the end table by her chair and gave it a single ring.

After a moment, the maid returned, carrying a long, polished wooden box. She laid it daintily on the coffee table in front of Carlee and Jasmina, curtseyed to Jasmina again, and shuffled away—not a word spoken.

"Here we are," Jasmina said, caressing the box's lines. "Your tools."

With a quick flick, a gesture laden with the elegance of having performed it thousands of times, the silver latch was undone. The care and reverence with which Jasmina handled the box reminded Carlee of how she handled the packages her computer video cards came in.

Jasmina's showmanship drew Carlee toward the box. She had never been to a dealer before, but she couldn't imagine this was how drugs were typically sold. Finally, Jasmina lifted the lid and revealed...

"Eyeshadow?" Carlee asked, raising an eyebrow and looking back up at Jasmina. The Duchess's smile was innocent, but Carlee could swear there was a hint of bemusement in it.

"The *best* eyeshadow," Jasmina said.

Had she given Jasmina the wrong phrase? No, Lula had set the meeting up to be a drug deal.

Maybe it's underneath? Carlee thought, picking up a palette and tentatively looking below it.

"I do not *stack* my product," Jasmina said, the mere thought a grave insult. "It is far too priceless for something so mundane as *stacking*."

"Of course. What was I thinking, Duchess?" Carlee said, trying to quell a nervous laugh.

"Do you have the goods?" Ian asked in her ear.

"This is all very lovely," Carlee said. "Do you have any *other* selections? I was thinking something a little more heavy-duty."

Jasmina laughed, her smile remaining innocent. "No, this is all I have. It should be more than enough for someone still making a name for themselves."

"I'm sure it is more than enough," Carlee said. "It's just, Lula mentioned you had some other options as well."

"Ah, yes, dear Lula," Jasmina said. "Tell me again how you met her? Certainly she wasn't trawling through... where was it—Shanghai?—when she found you."

Carlee checked another relieved sigh before it slipped out. She was ready for a question like this, had even practiced her answer several times last night. She wouldn't be blindsided.

"Oh, no, of course not," Carlee said, her voice even. "I was a student at Aphrodite. She was my favorite teacher, and—while I don't mean to speak for her—I like to think I was her favorite student."

"Isn't that wonderful," Jasmina said. "The relationship between pupil and instructor is a sacred one. I'm happy you two found each other."

"I was actually wondering..." Carlee said, seeing an opening. "A couple of other students Lula also took under her wing raved about being sent your way too, but I never believed it. They didn't have the quality you're obviously looking for in your customers."

Jasmina pursed her lips, making a show of considering the suggestion. "Hm. No, I don't recall Lula making any recommendations other than you."

"Are you sure? They described this place to a tee. Their names are Janie and Iris. Does that ring any bells?"

"As I said... Lula has never recommended any of her students before. I'll make sure you're the first and last since I don't want rumors like that to start spreading. Young ones like you couldn't even imagine what to do with some of my products."

"I hear you," Carlee said. Taking her phone out, she pulled up photos of both women and showed them to Jasmina. "You have a reputation to maintain, and being related to these two certainly can ruin it."

Jasmina leaned in and squinted at the small photos, and—no matter how hard the Duchess tried to hide it—Carlee could see a flash of awareness in her eyes, the little spark she had trained herself to never miss.

Eventually, Jasmina sat back in her chair, shaking her head. "Exactly. They don't appear to be the type of client who personally buys products from me," she said. "No offense."

"Cut your losses and get out," Zack said in Carlee's ear. "You're in the hot seat, we're getting squat, and I'm starting to get a bad feeling about—"

"Actually…" Jasmina stood up in a flash, startling Carlee. "Stay here while I retrieve something. I'll be right back."

Jasmina glided out of the room, leaving Carlee glued to her chair, her heart hammering, alarms wailing in her head.

"What the fuck do you think you're doing by pulling up those photos?" Ian fumed, though his furious voice sounded small in her ear. "This nutcase might be the Two-Faced Killer, and you show her pictures of her victims?"

"You're going off script, Carlee," Zack said, wrestling the mic from Ian. "Give Jasmina an excuse the second she gets back and get the hell out of there."

They were right. God damn it, they were right, but so was she. The Duchess *had* recognized at least one of the girls. Bare minimum, she knew Janie had gotten ahold of Jasmina's makeup…

She had barely stood up when the clicks of Jasmina's six-inch heels approached, and Carlee plopped back down just as she opened the door. Whatever it was she expected her host to return with—a needle of ketamine, a knife—it definitely wasn't what she held in her hands.

Jasmina walked into the room, a large stack of neatly aligned papers balanced in front of her. She unceremoniously dropped them onto the coffee table next to the box of makeup and retook her place on her throne, all without saying a word.

Carlee looked back and forth between the Duchess and the papers, but Jasmina offered no further prompting. She merely stared at her guest. Eventually, Carlee leaned in and plucked the top page from the stack, inspecting it before picking up the next and the next.

"These are—"

"Copies of every in-person sale I've made over the past year," Jasmina explained.

The papers were lined from top to bottom with dates, credit card numbers, and dollar amounts... but no names or descriptions of what was sold.

"I don't understand," Carlee stammered. "Why are you showing me this?"

"This is what you're here for, isn't it?" Jasmina asked innocently. "I know exactly who you are and what you want from me."

"Run!" Ian shouted into the mic. "Get out of there!"

"I'm sorry," Carlee tried, weakly, "but I don't think—"

"Drop the act, all right? I know you're working for that old hag." Jasmina stared daggers into her. "She's trying to point fingers and knock me out of the industry. She doesn't want to go quietly into retirement like she should, and she's clearly trying to make some big splash."

"Lula?" Carlee asked in true wonder.

"Yes, fucking Lula!" The surge of venom pouring from Jasmina contrasted dramatically with the regal and implacable manner she had held throughout their meeting. "I didn't want to believe it, which is why I agreed to meet with you, but now you can get the fuck out of my house and tell her she's dead to me. If she was ever alive to begin with."

"I'm—I'm sorry." She got up to leave, but as if to stamp her royal seal on the whole conversation, Jasmina leaned forward and tore at the front of Carlee's shirt, sending buttons flying across the room.

"And you can stop fidgeting while trying to hide this little thing—because I knew about it all along!" The Duchess reached into Carlee's shirt, grabbed the wire, and ripped it free.

Chapter Eighteen

Zack West had weathered a lot of storms throughout his career—and been chewed out by more than one superior. Hell, he'd been chewed out by his superior's superiors more times than he could count. He had even once earned the personal ire of the chief of police after he had borrowed his fancy German sports car to pursue a suspect.

In Zack's defense, though, the chief *had* double parked behind his squad car.

"Are you absolutely out of your goddamned mind, West?" Marisol's voice boomed off the walls, making the detectives at the far end of the bullpen wince.

For all the tongue lashings he'd withstood in the past, no one could lash quite like Marisol Shae. Zack knew that Marisol's small frame belied a fire that burned hotter than everyone else's combined. Part of what made her an excellent commander was her ability to control it.

She wasn't making any attempt to control it now.

"Do you have any idea how much of a complete asshole you made of me this morning?" she screamed, pacing back and forth in front of him.

Zack stood there quietly. He knew from hard-earned experience that answering her before she got her anger out was the exact wrong thing to do.

"The chief sat right there—in my office—for twenty minutes, West." Marisol's face was shifting from pink to maroon. Zack knew that one shade darker meant she'd be done. "We were there for twenty minutes, sitting with our thumbs up our asses. Waiting for you. Do you know how many times I had to tell him you were just about to show up?"

This was not a rhetorical question. "Three times, ma'am?"

"*Five times*, West!" Marisol held out her hand, all fingers outstretched, an inch from his face. "That's every four minutes! And that's not including having to tell him we'd need to reschedule!"

There it was, the plum shade that meant it was his turn to try and talk her down. "I can't apologize enough, ma'am, although—"

"No. You're right. You can't. Do you understand how bad it makes me look as a commander when my goddamned detectives can't even be assed to make a meeting with the chief?"

"That's not on you, ma'am. That's on me," Zack proffered with what he hoped was the right amount of humility. It was the wrong thing to say, and he knew it the second he said it.

"That's your *fucking* problem, West." She prowled up close to him, her voice low. Zack couldn't help but feel like a deer in front of a mountain lion. "You're not a one-man show. Your actions reflect on the whole department. Reflect on *me*." She took a deep breath and stepped back.

"It won't—" Zack started.

"Don't," Marisol cut him off again. "You can start to make it up to me by telling me you were too busy working the Eighth-Grade Killer case and time just *happened* to slip by."

"No, ma'am, I wasn't," he said. This was bait and he knew it. Marisol knew well enough that Zack hadn't been working the Eighth-Grade Killer case that morning, but she wanted him to admit it.

"And what, pray tell, was so important that you weren't working on the one case I've assigned to you?" Marisol asked, pinching the bridge of her nose.

"The Two-Faced Killer case."

"The Two-Faced Killer case!?" she bugled, shaking the bull pen's attention again. "Can anyone tell me what precinct has been assigned the Two-Faced Killer case?"

There was a moment of silence before one of the other detectives piped up weakly. "Second Precinct, ma'am."

"Now tell me, Detective West," Marisol continued through gritted teeth. "Are we the Second Precinct?"

"No, ma'am."

"Did we get redesignated while I wasn't looking?"

"No, ma'am."

"Then why the hell are you working a case that isn't yours," Marisol said, no longer needing to yell to convey how angry she was, "when you already have an incredibly important case assigned to you?"

This was a rhetorical question. Zack knew—again, from hard-earned experience—that the last thing he should do is try to explain himself now. He was out of the danger zone, but only just. If Marisol had any idea that he had skipped the meeting to participate in an unsanctioned sting with an FBI agent and a private investigator, she would've skinned him right then and there and nailed his pelt to the wall as a warning to the other detectives.

Best to say nothing, then.

Marisol turned to stalk back to her office, and Zack followed her. She glared at him but otherwise didn't tell him to piss off. The other detectives returned to their work, intuiting that the public flogging was over for the moment.

"Believe me, ma'am. The Janie Toland case is relevant to my investigation," Zack said, keeping his tone low so it would stay between them. "And if you'd allow me to follow my hunch here, I think I might actually find something worthy of a meeting with the chief."

Marisol didn't reply—only opened the door to her office, allowing him to follow her through. Then she closed it, giving them some privacy.

"Cut the bullshit, Detective," she said, her tone returning to its typical even keel. "You haven't been in the office all damn day. I know this because the manilla envelope with the fingerprint data has been lying—unopened—on your desk since ten o'clock this morning."

Zack winced. He had just started going over the contents of the packet when Marisol had stormed up to his desk. From what he had seen, the CSU guys had run the partial print found on Joel's button against inmates who had just completed thirteen-year sentences, looking for matches with their bare-bones profile of the Eighth-Grade Killer. It was a total shot in the dark, and Zack didn't have great hopes that it would get them any answers.

"Zack, I am *this* close to handing the Eighth-Grade Killer case to someone else." She held up her hand, thumb and forefinger practically touching. "If you don't get your fucking act together—if you don't shape the fuck up—I'm going to bench you."

"Ma'am, I'm just—"

"I don't want to hear any more of your excuses, Zack," Marisol said, deflating back into her chair. "I understand you've got personal shit that you're dealing with. I cut you some slack during your divorce, didn't I? But what the fuck is your excuse now?"

"I don't have an excuse, ma'am," Zack said, standing at attention. "I'm focused on my current assignment, but I really do think the cases are related. You don't have to worry about me. I just need to dig a little deeper, and if I see that they're not related, I'll—"

"I always have to worry about you," Marisol said, the barest hint of a smile betraying her. "You're lucky you usually get shit done."

"Yes, ma'am," Zack said. He knew these were the words he had to say to ensure she wouldn't boot him from the Eighth-Grade Killer case, and he was willing to say them.

"Okay, Detective," Marisol said. "You've bought yourself some time. Now, if I might suggest, get out there and use it wisely."

"Of course, Commander."

She nodded to him, signaling his dismissal, and he turned to leave the office. He would be damned before he gave up the Eighth-Grade Killer case, but he also had no plans of stopping his current investigation. He'd just have to be a little more careful in how he went about it.

As he approached his desk, his cell phone began to buzz in his pocket. Fishing it out, he checked the caller ID. Mercycrest—the hospital where Iris was currently recuperating. He answered immediately.

"Hello, Detective West?" Khalil, Iris's doctor, asked on the other end. Even through the phone, Zack could hear the dread in his voice.

"Yes," Zack gasped, his heart beating faster. "What is it? Is Iris all right?"

Khalil sighed deeply. "Well, no. Iris coded a few minutes ago. She's gone."

And with that, so was their best lead.

Chapter Nineteen

Her mind raced as she flipped through page after page of digital documents, but Carlee's brain refused to remember a single pertinent fact.

"Carlee," Zack's voice came in from the phone. She had put him on speaker, not sure if it was because she was unable or unwilling to hold it next to her ear. "Did you hear me?"

"Yeah, yes," she mumbled, shaking her head, trying to clear her thoughts. Iris was dead, and she was still trying to process the new wrinkle in the case.

No, not 'wrinkle,' she chided herself in the back of her head. *Somebody died*.

The worst part was that her immediate reaction to Zack's news hadn't been sadness. She hadn't hoped that Iris's family raced back to Chicago to see her one last time. No, Carlee's first thought had been an angry one—she had lost such a strong and promising lead.

Now she sat at her desk, flipping through files on her computer, an old feeling of disgust settling over her. And Zack West was still harping away on speaker, not allowing her to stew in her burgeoning self-hatred.

"The doctor said losing her was a distinct possibility," he reminded her. "It's not like it came out of left field."

"No, it didn't," Carlee conceded. It would do Iris's memory no good to simmer in loathing. More than ever, she needed to stow her ego, find who did this, and drag them to justice. "But that doesn't make it sting less, Zack. I didn't think it would be this soon. Hell, you saw her yourself! She looked bad, yeah, but she didn't look like she was hanging on by a damned thread!"

"These things can happen," Zack insisted, his voice somewhere between consoling and stern. "I saw it all the time on my old beat when I was a uniform. Heavy users pay a heavy price. It's a terrible thing, but it happens."

"I just wish I could have talked to her one more time," Carlee said. "I'm sure she could've helped us blow this whole thing wide open."

Zack sighed. "I know. Me too. The real world rarely works that way, though."

Carlee closed her eyes for a moment. "How are we going to nail Jasmina now?"

"Easier asked than answered, Carlee."

The Duchess turned out to be far slipperier than expected. They knew she was dealing, but the documents she had given them—Zack had already traced the credit card numbers, which Carlee was now perusing—proved nothing. At most, they proved Jasmina's clients were all involved in fashion, which was about as helpful as it sounded.

"I'm not seeing Janie or Iris on any of these lists," Carlee said, scrolling through the pages.

"That's because they're not," Zack griped. "They were the first names I looked for. Worse, there isn't a single person on the list who's been picked up on a drug charge. She wasn't lying. She knew someone was listening and she was very careful."

"You're not trying to say the Duchess is *really* just a makeup dealer, are you?" Carlee groaned, pulling out a desk drawer and digging out her trusty bottle of ibuprofen, desperate to fight off a building headache. She threw two into her mouth and washed them down with a gulp of water. "Please tell me I'm not living in some screwed-up dreamworld where everyone else thinks that 'interview' was normal..."

"Absolutely not," Zack said. "There's enough circumstantial evidence that her business isn't really in question. Unfortunately for us, warrants aren't signed on circumstantial evidence."

Jasmina had gone to great lengths to keep her record spotless, to stay above suspicion. Not a single arrest, not a single run-in with the law, not a single known associate involved in the drug trade. She curated and vetted all of her clients—both legal and illicit—with a process that made her functionally bulletproof. As a result, there wasn't a judge in all of Cook County who would sign off on a warrant.

Ian's voice whispered in the back of her mind again, making her wonder if Zack was going about this the right way. Carlee hated that she was now questioning Zack's adherence to procedure through the paranoid lens Ian had slipped over her eye. She shouldn't be second-guessing good police work...

"But we know Janie had access to Facade by Jaq Curwood," Carlee said, adopting the snobbiest accent she could affect. She even lifted a pinky as she said the brand name. "Where would she have gotten it if not from Jasmina?"

Zack grunted. "That's the million-dollar question, isn't it?"

"You don't think they used cash, do you?" Carlee asked, the thought of physical cash in her digital world almost as archaic as pirate doubloons. "I would say it's more likely they got the makeup from someone else. I doubt she keeps her drug sales in neatly indexed documents."

"That would seem unlikely," Zack agreed. "But we need to focus on how we're going to nail her on it."

Carlee hummed as she scrolled through more documents. A nagging thought, one that had begun to grow since her meeting with Jasmina, came to the forefront. Throughout their entire interaction, even when Jasmina had pulled the wire from her blouse—the damage to which she was still trying to figure out how she would explain to Eleanor—she had struck Carlee as more of a businesswoman than a serial killer.

Would the Two-Faced Killer have let her walk out of her home after spotting a wire? Backup or not, Carlee imagined that situation would have played out much differently if Jasmina had been a bloodthirsty murderer.

"You're not going to like this, Zack," Carlee told him, shaking her head, "but I think we might be focusing on the wrong person. I don't think Jasmina is our killer."

Zack sighed. "Of course you don't."

"I mean it, Zack."

"All right, Carlee. I'll humor you. Tell me what you're thinking."

"I still think Jasmina had plenty of motive to harm Janie," she insisted, her thoughts snowballing. "Especially after that video of her tearing into Jaq Curwood went viral. Tons of people in the industry were talking about it and Jasmina doesn't strike me as someone who would just let something like that slide."

"I'm sensing a 'but' here."

"But she had no motive to harm Iris," Carlee said. "You said it yourself, Zack. Jasmina only deals with the rich and famous. You could argue that Janie was on her way to becoming an influencer, but Iris was a complete nobody. She was going back and forth between nursing school and Aphrodite. She didn't have the time to be rich *or* famous."

"I smell what you're cooking, I guess. How the hell would Iris have gotten an in with an exclusive, high-end, royal drug dealer in the first place?"

"I don't think she did," Carlee said, her gaze drifting back to the list of names and numbers. "There's something we're missing here."

"Well, we need to figure it out fast or I'm out of a job!"

"Hold on," Carlee said as her fingers flew across her keyboard. She dragged each of the files into a custom investigation program she'd developed, and it immediately began collating the information while she ran a hacking script on the Aphrodite administration website.

In moments, Carlee had a complete record of faculty, staff, and students. She dropped them into the program, which began matching data points.

"I don't know if this is worth holding your breath over, but I might just have a hunch growing."

"And that hunch would be...?"

"I've just made a nice, neat list of matches between Jasmina's clients and anyone associated with Aphrodite," Carlee said. "None of them are Two-Faced Killer victims, but Jasmina was—is—quite popular at the school."

"And why is that remarkable? It makes sense she'd want to keep an eye on upcoming talent," Zack figured. "An easy way to stay relevant, if nothing else. So it stands to reason that the Duchess would be a popular source of makeup and drugs with the Chicago scene."

"You're still stuck on Jasmina as the killer," Carlee said simply.

"So you think she's unrelated?"

"Maybe not completely unrelated. Consider this: What if she *is* the Two-Faced Killer's supplier? A poisoner has to get their ketamine from somewhere, so why not from the same pool they pull their targets?"

Zack mulled it over. "It's possible," he admitted begrudgingly, "but we need more evidence before we can chase it."

"Is *my* gut feeling not enough for you, West?" she sassed, fighting off a smile.

"Normally, yes," Zack said. She could hear a smile of his own. "But given my current, uh, job security status... I need to tread lightly."

"So, what do you propose?" Carlee asked, looking over the list of Jasmina's Aphrodite clients. "I say we need to get to—"

"—the school and check it out ourselves," he finished for her.

Carlee's body thrummed with the anticipation, of the second lap of the chase. She was about to schedule a visit to Aphrodite when a buzz cut into her focus. Picking up her phone, she saw it was an incoming call from Ian.

"Ah, shit. Hey, give me a second, would you?"

"Sure thing," Zack said.

She put him on hold and switched over to Ian. "This will have to be fast, Garnett. And I mean no-detours fast. I'm in the middle of something big."

"Not bigger than this, I assure you," Ian said, his easygoing confidence oozing through the phone. "I've got a scoop so fresh, your best friend Zack doesn't even know about it yet."

"Is that so?" Carlee didn't know why, but her body steeled itself. "Well, by all means... please fill me in on this *bigger-than-yours* news that can't wai—"

"There's another victim," Ian snapped.

"Matching which of the killers' MO?" Carlee asked, dreading his answer.

"She's all dressed up, made-up, posed, and her throat's been cut. The Two-Faced Killer is officially at three new victims."

Carlee's heart dropped into her stomach as her headache roared to life.

Chapter Twenty

Carlee had never been prone to motion sickness. She always thought it was weird when Cameron complained that he couldn't read on long family car trips, but as she flipped through the new crime scene photos in the back of Zack's car, she felt a little like she was going to lose her breakfast.

"These aren't the first crime scene photos I've seen," Carlee swore, fighting down a wave of nausea. She caught a worried flash of Zack's eyes in the rearview mirror. "Not even close. They're not even the most gruesome."

Ian twisted around in the passenger seat and leaned over the back. "I know."

"So why is it that these make me want to roll the window down and vomit out the side?" Carlee asked him.

"It's the nature of the crime and how it looks in the CSU photos," he explained, tapping the photo in front of her. "Because the victim is posed the way she is, regardless of what the crime scene photographer shoots, it ends up looking like some sort of gory fashion magazine spread. And it's sickening."

The victim, Yolanda Bradley, had been found in her garage, draped over the hood of her car, her throat slit. Her clothing—a too-tight tank top decorated with rhinestone gems, a too-loose pleather skirt, and knee-high patent leather platform boots—plus amateurishly airbrushed makeup and messy hair gave her the look of a parody hotrod pinup model. To the surprise of no one in the car, she was a student at Aphrodite.

"It's still exceptionally fucking sick if you ask me," Zack said, gripping the steering wheel. He had pointedly kept all of his attention on the road as he drove to Aphrodite.

"Agreed," Carlee said, flipping to the next photo. She scoured every inch for a potentially missed clue. "You're telling me these don't make you just a little queasy, Ian?"

"I didn't go over them in the back of a swerving vehicle," Ian said. "Not that you're swerving, big guy. You're doing great." Without turning back, he slapped Zack's shoulder.

Zack tensed up behind the wheel, and Carlee imagined if Ian had tried that while he wasn't driving, his wrist would've been snapped.

Instead, Zack cricked his neck and ignored the jab, pulling the car into a parking spot down the road from the beauty institute. "We're here."

Carlee wasted no time getting out. The city air, cooled by the Chicago River flowing a few blocks away, was fresh compared to the cramped confines of Zack's car. Centering herself, she looked over the brick buildings clustered on the block, a string of properties that formed Aphrodite Institute.

"It's no coincidence that all three victims attended this school," Carlee said, primarily to herself. "Something happened here that led to the murders, and I'm going to figure out what."

Zack locked the car and joined them on the sidewalk. They took a moment to watch students and staff walk in and out of Aphrodite's doors. Carlee hoped her insistence that Ian tag along to lend them some official FBI clout wouldn't backfire in another blowup.

"Most of these kids probably aren't old enough to remember the original Two-Faced killings," Ian mused. He wasn't wrong. The average age of enrollees was midtwenties; the oldest were babies during the Two-Faced Killer's initial reign. "If we're looking for copycat candidates, they would be makeup artists who know about a thirty-year-old mystery. They might've chosen the Two-Faced Killer's techniques to send a message."

"I'm not sure we're after a copycat anymore," Carlee said. "If we include Iris—and there's no reason we shouldn't at this point—each of the three victims exhibited the Two-Faced Killer's MO to the letter, minus the change in drug choice."

Zack nodded. "I agree. A copycat could spend hours obsessing over the details but still mess up something small. Not our killer."

"Do you two ever listen to yourselves?" Ian asked, ignoring the death stare Zack gave him. "You're chasing your tails. It's standard FBI procedure: The best way to handle an investigation like this is from the top down. We talk with the school's president and piggyback off whatever internal investigation they're undoubtedly doing. This is shit we learned at Quantico."

"Did you learn how to get your ass kicked at Quantico too?" Zack snapped.

"Oh, no... Officer Friendly seems upset," Ian noted, his toothy grin visibly pushing Zack's buttons harder. "Eventually you'll learn that some things are out of your depth. Nothing wrong with it. It's just the food chain."

Carlee spotted Zack's fist tightening in his pocket. The subtle turn in his shoulders told her all she needed to know—if she didn't do something, they'd end up wasting precious time taking Ian to the hospital to get his split lip stitched.

"That's enough," Carlee shouted, physically putting herself between them. "Stop acting like goddamned children!" She stormed off toward the school, not bothering to look back. If they wanted to get into a fight on a sidewalk before ten in the morning, fine by her, but she would have nothing to do with it.

Carlee supposed she was relieved to hear two distinct huffs, followed by the clapping footsteps of two men jogging to catch up to her.

They walked into the lobby together, beelining for the administration office. Before they could put together a game plan, however, Ian strolled ahead of them. He pivoted on his heel, facing them while walking backward.

"You two stay here," he said, his grin implacable. "And let the FBI handle this."

Once the office door closed and Ian was out of earshot, Zack growled, "I'm sorry, Carlee. I know he's your friend or whatever, but I fucking hate that guy. I will tase his ass to shut him up if I have to. And that's not a warning, it's a goddamned promise!"

"He can be a bit much sometimes, I know," Carlee admitted as diplomatically as she could. "But he's a hell of an investigator."

"I've met guys like him before," Zack said, his face clouding. "Guys who join up because they want the swagger that comes with the badge and the gun. They're usually high school bullies who got upset that they couldn't be bullies when they became adults. So they do this job because they like the power, not because they want to help people."

"Maybe you're right in general, but not about Ian. He's helped me many times in the past. He's the only reason I didn't get carved alive in Harborside during the Caldwell case."

"I actually read up on that case," Zack said. "It sounded like you had a good handle on it without him."

"And here I believed you thought I couldn't handle myself in these kinds of situations."

"I think you can handle yourself just fine, but shit hits the fan sometimes," Zack said, pulling one of Carlee's black curls back to reveal the scar under her ear where Justin Winslow had nearly slit her carotid. The scar had long since stopped hurting, though it still itched now and then.

Carlee flattened her hair back into place. "I know he's an asshole, but I owe him my life, Zack. So, if you could do me a favor, could you give him even the slightest benefit of the doubt?"

Ian opened the doors to the office and peeked out, motioning for them to follow. Zack sighed. It sounded old and weathered.

"Fine," he said, leaning toward Carlee as they approached the office. "I'll give Agent Asshole a shot. But if he calls me 'Officer Friendly' again, I'll teach him some of the hand-to-hand we learned at the academy."

"If it comes to that, I'll hold him down for you," Carlee whispered to Zack as Ian waved them to the receptionist's desk.

"I'm pleased to inform you," Ian said, "that Carol, here—"

"Karyn," the receptionist feebly tried to correct him.

"—told me that the president was incredibly busy but could make some time for an FBI agent."

"Of course," Carlee said, reining in her annoyance. "So they'll see us now?"

"They'll see *me* now, actually," Ian corrected her, his smile apologetic.

"Excuse me?" Zack squawked. Carlee could almost feel the heat of his temper flaring. "You're already cutting us out?"

"I wouldn't say 'cutting you out' as much as I'd say 'setting you free,'" Ian said. If he weren't an FBI agent, Carlee imagined Ian would've been the best used-car salesman in the entire state of Illinois. "Interviewing a president about a case? That's a one-man job. I'll talk, and you two split up and question some professors. Cover more ground."

There was a pause, and Carlee was worried Zack might consider punching Ian again, but he surprised her. "Good idea," he gritted out. "Let's do that."

"Excellent." Ian clapped his hands together as if he were in charge of the operation. "Let's get to work, team."

Once Carlee and Zack were back out in the lobby, she turned to him. "You know, I was actually kind of hoping you'd tase him for that."

He managed a quirk of a smile. "Don't give up on your dreams just yet."

They began to make their way down the hall, leaving the front office behind.

"So, you agree with Agent Asshole for once, huh?"

"Splitting up makes sense. We do need to cover more ground, but I don't understand how he manages to make a good idea piss me off so much."

Carlee tapped her chin. "A lot of practice, I think," she said.

Zack glanced back toward the administration office. "I just hope he has more tact when dealing with officials."

Ian was an ass, true, but Carlee had never known him to jeopardize an investigation because of it, and she didn't think he was about to start now. "He's probably trying to run a smoke screen for us," she told him, thinking out loud.

Zack snorted. "I doubt that."

"No, trust me. He took the metaphorical bullet so we could do some actual investigating. I don't suspect he'll get anything more than boilerplate PR answers out of the president."

"I cannot imagine that man doing anything altruistic," Zack said, a sneer on his lip. "Still, I'd rather be out here working with you than in there schmoozing with him."

As they walked down the hall, the difference between the Aphrodite of their last visit and the Aphrodite of the present was stunning. There were no students taking selfies and no instructors running to make it to their classes on time. It was as if the institute had transformed into a ghost town.

"I suppose they canceled classes," Zack said, peeking into an empty room.

"Makes sense," Carlee agreed. She thought back to Harborside and how the junior high administration thought canceling classes might help keep students safe. It hadn't. She shuddered. "It won't make our job any easier, though."

In the distance, three doors away, a soft conversation wafted out of a classroom. Zack and Carlee approached it stealthily, as if they might spook the room's inhabitants.

Carlee poked her head around the threshold and saw two teachers sitting close together, whispering, their faces bent toward each other.

Zack peeked his head over hers. "Sorry to interrupt," he said, walking inside. He pulled his badge off his hip and held it out. "My name is Detective Zack West, and this is my colleague, Carlee Knight. We were wondering if we could ask you some questions?"

The instructors eyed them suspiciously before one finally nodded. "I guess that'd be okay. I take it you're here about Janie?"

"And Iris. And Yolanda," the other added. "Jesus."

"Yes, that's exactly why we're here," Carlee said, keeping her tone soft and placating. She could see these women were holding onto their calm by a thread. "Do you know if the school administration has been investigating any of the teachers here at Aphrodite?"

The two teachers peered at each other. She had apparently hit a touchy subject. That meant it had been the right question to ask.

"We have no clue what's going on," one of them finally said. "They're keeping a tight lid on everything. Keeping us out of the loop."

"Which is fucking crazy," the other snapped. "How do they expect us to do our jobs when there's a fucking serial killer out there targeting us?"

"Could this killer be a faculty member?" Zack asked.

"God, I hope not," one said. She shook her head and shivered at the thought. "I can't imagine it, no. But who the hell knows? This industry—and this school—has attracted some absolute whack-a-doodles."

"That's unfair," the other cut in. "I've been here for decades, and we've never had issues with on-campus violence."

"On-campus violence?" the first one retorted. "Three students were brutally killed!"

"I'm sure it's not related to Aphrodite. Admin is just trying to cover their own ass."

"Cover their own ass? Are you kidding me? There's a *serial killer* on the loose."

The instructors devolved into bickering, the stress of the last few days running through them like cracks on an egg.

"Again, I hate to interrupt," Zack said, trying his best to cut in. "But could you tell me if there's been any sort of flare-up with the staff recently? Any drama?"

His questions landed on deaf ears. The teachers, entirely embroiled in their own theories, left it hanging. Carlee was about to step in and give wrangling the instructors a shot when her phone buzzed—a text.

Unknown: "Is this Carlee Knight?"

Carlee furrowed her brow and regarded the message only for a moment before she replied.

Carlee: "Who's asking?"

Unknown: "Someone with information."

Carlee: "Does 'someone with information' have a name?"

Unknown: "I don't want to say over the phone, but I promise this is legit. Can we meet up?"

Carlee: "I'm not in the habit of meeting with strangers. We can talk as soon as you tell me who you are."

Carlee chewed her lip, watching the dots blink as *Unknown* typed their response.

Unknown: "Please, I need to talk to you. I know who killed Yolanda, and I think I know who's next!"

Chapter Twenty-One

Her skin crawled and her mind raced. It wasn't because the apartment Carlee was currently in was old and dilapidated—that didn't bother her at all. What bothered her was how entirely, dismally insecure everything was.

The moment Carlee arrived, Sofia—the mysterious Aphrodite student who'd texted her while she and Zack skulked around the school—had ushered her into a shabby living room and away from the front door, unwilling to discuss Yolanda's death where someone might listen in.

Even now, as they sat opposite one another at a little folding table better suited for playing cards, Sofia kept her voice low and conspiratorial, explaining the strange circumstances of her friend's murder.

Their short conversation on the phone earlier revealed that Sofia was genuinely afraid for her life. Carlee knew Zack and Ian's intense questioning style would trample this fragile girl like energetic dogs set loose in a sprouting garden, so she'd decided to come alone.

"It was last year. That's why this is all happening," Sofia said, her button nose bunched up in concern. "I told them they were going too far!"

"Let's start from the beginning," Carlee suggested. "Who's 'them'? What were they doing?"

"Them! The girls! I tried to stop them, but they said it was all a joke."

"All right, Sofia, I need you to slow down a little," Carlee said, placing a calming hand on Sofia's knee. "I know you're scared to tell me about this. Believe me, I completely understand what that feels like, so let's just take it one sentence at a time."

She took some exaggeratedly deep breaths, and Sofia followed suit, though telling this girl to "calm down" with so much authority made Carlee feel like a fraud. Her mind was still wound tight with the dread of her stalker's last threat, and no matter how hard she tried to focus, the front door kept drawing her eyes away.

"You said it all started last year?"

"Yes. With the competition."

"And what competition was that?"

"It was put on by a local company so they could use Chicago talent in their marketing campaign," Sofia explained pausing to chew on her thumbnail. "All the big beauty institutes in the city participated."

"Tell me more. Was it a competition for students?" Carlee asked.

A soft clack at the door made both of them jump, but it was merely the mailman pushing an envelope through the mail slot. Their eyes met in the silence, and they shared an anxious laugh at their own expense.

"I think my nervousness is spreading," Sofia admitted sheepishly, then forged ahead before the fear could get its claws into her again. "The competition wasn't for students, but for the faculty. They invented these *super* experimental looks... kind of like painting a portrait on someone's face, you know? Aphrodite poured, like, a ton of marketing into it."

"I think I'm following. If one of their teachers won, it would be crazy good for enrollment, right?"

"Right, and the *students* got to critique everything online," Sofia said, her finger stabbing the air to emphasize the point. "We were all basically the judges. We ranked each of the looks, and we could also leave comments."

"Sounds fun," Carlee supposed, unconvinced it did. "And you think that had something to do with Yolanda's death?"

"I'm getting there," Sofia said. "You have to understand. This campaign was a capital-B, capital-D *Big Deal*. A lot of the teachers at Aphrodite could've used the exposure of winning, landing one of their looks in a major ad campaign. We're talking magazine spreads, posters everywhere, billboards downtown..."

"Hold on, I think I remember that," Carlee said, snapping her fingers to try and jog her memory. "It was around Christmas. Those weird billboards where half of it was just white, and the other half was a pair of orange lips or, uh... a single made-up eye or something?"

"That's the one!" Sofia said, her face lighting up.

"I remember thinking it was a weird campaign."

"I suppose somebody like you would, but to people in the industry, it was huge. Life or death."

"I'll take your word for it," Carlee said, barely caring about the subtle insult of the phrase *somebody like you*. "Now, how does this have anything to do with the Two-Faced Killer?"

"Remember how I said the students got to rate and critique the looks?" Sofia grimaced. "Well, Yolanda and Iris took that as a challenge."

"Meaning they critiqued a lot?"

"'A lot' doesn't get to the half of it," Sofia whispered. "They absolutely *tore* into the Aphrodite teachers. Stuff like, 'I didn't know my blind niece taught at Aphrodite' and 'RIP to the teacher who had a seizure halfway through this look.'"

"Damn! That's brutal." Carlee winced, imagining some little brat tearing into her pride-and-joy drones that way.

Sofia sighed. "That's not even the worst of it. They got absolutely vile. It was like the two of them thought this was their chance at revenge against the school for some reason. Their flame war got so bad, even some students from other institutes told them to lay off. It totally sunk Aphrodite's chance of winning. Not a single one of our teachers got picked, not even for an honorable mention, and they were *pissed*."

"Who got pissed, exactly? Can you give me names, projects, classes?" Carlee asked, leaning in to make sure she didn't miss anything. "Does anyone stand out more than the others?"

"Vinny was out of his mind about it." Sofia closed her eyes as if finally speaking the name out loud reinforced her certainty. "Vinny Garrard."

Carlee's mouth fell ajar as she recalled her chat with Vinny Garrard in his office. He had seemed upbeat, calm, and eager to share his cosmetics expertise—if a little condescending. Had they unwittingly consulted the Two-Faced Killer about his own crime?

"Do you have any proof, Sofia?" she asked. "Anything that could give me some idea of how angry he was about this?"

"Like what?"

"I don't know... social media posts, class announcements, angry emails or anything like that?"

"Oh, you bet I do." Sofia pulled her phone from her housecoat pocket to show Carlee page after page of emails, each of them forwarded to a host of sympathetic students from the late Yolanda Bradley. "Look at all this bullshit. And this is just what Yolanda forwarded us from her chats with the dean. Who knows what Vinny said to the president behind closed doors?"

"So it was mostly Vinny making remarks to Yolanda and Iris? Did he actually take action against them somehow?"

Sofia shrugged, continuing to scroll. "I don't know specifically what he did, but from what Iris told me, one thing is clear: he tried really hard to get both of them expelled."

"As in...?"

"As in he told the administration they had done 'irreparable harm to the reputation of the school and its staff' or something like that."

"So what did the administration do about it?"

"Fuck all! They said they weren't going to expel anyone over a critique, thank god," Sofia said. She handed the phone to Carlee, having found what she was looking for. "But they did send out this email. Here, read it for yourself."

Carlee took the phone and read, her eyes narrowing.

The faculty and staff here at the Aphrodite Beauty Institute are disheartened by the comments made in the most recent sponsorship competition. While we hope everyone at Aphrodite strives to support one another as we build toward future success, we would like to remind our community that fair criticism is an integral part of the arts. Administration will not take formal disciplinary action against critics at any level of the industry, though we are disappointed by the vitriolic nature of the criticism recently issued within our Aphrodite family. Please understand that networking is crucial to your longevity as a professional and that those you meet within our halls—faculty and students alike—are your largest network as you start your professional journey.

Sofia leaned back. "Harsh, right?"

"I'd say. And I assume Vinny did *not* like that," Carlee said, shaking her head.

"No, he did not. The asshole even yelled at Yolanda and Iris in class, in front of his other students."

"What did they do?"

"What do you think? They stormed out," Sofia snapped, "and went straight to the office about it. They dropped the class and got a refund, and Vinny had to apologize to *them*."

"So that's why you think he's involved? I mean, I see where you're coming from. Any teacher would hate being humiliated like that," Carlee agreed. "But I'm not sure it's motive for murder."

"You don't get it!" Sofia's voice rose, her fear of eavesdroppers forgotten. "He saw those posters and billboards all winter... and he saw Yolanda and Iris just going on with their lives, trotting around shows and exhibitions." She walloped her palm on the rickety table for emphasis, startling Carlee.

"Still, I'm not sure that's enough for him to snap."

"I am."

"Thing is," Carlee pressed, trying to calm Sofia as much as herself, "there's a victim unaccounted for. Does the name Janie Toland mean anything to you?"

Sofia shrugged. "I didn't know Janie apart from seeing her in the hall sometimes."

"Did you hear anything about her? Were there rumors about her being involved in this incident at all?"

"No, but maybe she did something else that pissed Vinny off. Because I know Yolanda and Iris were scared of him after that."

"Scared? Why? Did they tell you anything that made you think they were scared of revenge?"

"Not exactly about revenge, but... listen," Sofia said, looking almost embarrassed. "Yolanda and I spent a ton of time together these last few months, and me and Iris go way back. I *know* her. Knew her," she corrected herself, voice cracking.

"You knew her from before Aphrodite?"

"Yeah. Which is why I know something was wrong. We started nursing school together, and we got to be best friends." Sofia gave her a mournful smile. And, Carlee thought, maybe a smile that was a little envious too. "She was so good at everything she did."

"Wait—are you telling me you both did double duty at nursing school *and* beauty school?" Carlee asked warily, remembering what Iris had done to her body to keep up with her schedule.

"Hell no," Sofia chuckled. She looked away briefly, as if debating whether to go into detail. "I flunked out of nursing school in the first semester."

"Was starting up at Aphrodite your idea or Iris's?"

"Mine," Sofia said a little too quickly. "Iris followed me after I told her about it."

"I've talked with a lot of teachers at Aphrodite," Carlee said, playing on a hunch. "They all had nothing but good things to say about Iris. She was acing all her classes."

"I'm not surprised." Sofia's smile grew a hint tighter. "Iris was special."

"But I know being smart wasn't the full story, was it?" Carlee pushed, deciding not to tiptoe around taboos when there was a murderer on the loose.

Sofia grimaced, her eyebrows turning up, her lips turning down. "What do you... um... that's not really..."

"Did I mention that I was the one who found her?" Carlee added, hoping it would help Sofia understand there was no need to defend her late friend's honor. "I was at the hospital with her too. I spoke to her doctor."

"So...?"

"So you don't have to cover anything up. I know she was a heavy user."

"I kept telling her she should stop." The words spilled out of Sofia, crumbling her dam of emotions. She shook her head, dropping her face into her hands. "She would always tell me, 'just 'til I finish my classes.' That was Iris for you. She thought she knew everything, and she wasn't going to listen to some dropout."

Carlee's ears perked at the derision in Sofia's voice. Maybe the ketamine hadn't solely been a practical matter. What if it had been another means of shaming the Two-Faced Killer's victims, just like the clownish makeup?

"I got the impression Iris was a little cocky, yeah," Carlee said, gently leading her to reveal any hidden feelings—maybe even feelings Sofia herself didn't know she had.

"Oh, she was," Sofia said, bobbing her head, relieved she didn't have to be the one to say it. "It, um... feels wrong to criticize her when she can't defend herself. Though it wasn't so bad. It was all part of her charm."

"I'm sure it wasn't easy having your best friend living up to everything you failed to do."

"She was basically me but better. Though I loved her for it. Most of the time..."

"Well, you shouldn't feel bad, since you didn't need drugs to cope," Carlee said. Truthfully, she didn't give a damn about easing Sofia's insecurity—she needed to earn her trust.

"Iris was so laissez-faire about everything," Sofia said, getting worked up. She was clearly itching to work off the energy of something she'd bottled up for far too long. "It was like she didn't think anything of putting that poison into her body. Told me I should take pills too if I didn't want to fail..."

Carlee snorted. "Wow. That would have pissed me the hell off." She folded her arms and leaned back in the cheap chair. "It must've made you want to give her a piece of your mind."

At the height of her anger, Sofia slumped, the hot spark that had flared in her a second ago bleeding out.

"We had our ups and downs. But she was my best friend," Sofia swore, truly exhausted by the weight of her frustration, obviously ashamed of herself for letting it slip. "She stayed up with me every night at the end of that first semester of nursing school, trying to make sure I passed my finals."

Carlee sighed. If anyone was an authority on how difficult keeping—or even making—friends could be, it was her. She could count hers on one hand, and only two of those fingers were living beings and not machines. "I get it. You can love someone and want to slap the shit out of them at the same time."

"She could be an ice-cold bitch sometimes," Sofia said, laughing, the sound bittersweet. "She loved to gossip and talk shit behind people's backs. I do too, if I'm being honest. But it didn't matter how much we got in each other's faces. I knew at the end of the day she had my back, and she knew I had hers."

"Was Iris ever—"

"Like this one time," Sofia cut her off, her eyes lighting up at the memory, "I was running late for Lula Alford's class. Usually, Lula was pretty chill about that sort of thing, but I was *late* late."

"So what did you do?" Carlee played along.

"Well, *I* didn't do shit, but Iris came up with this whole story about how my uncle had gone into surgery—used that nursing school knowledge, you know? Made it sound all official. By the time I got to class, Lula told me I shouldn't have even come in, but she was 'so impressed by my strength and persistence.' I think I even got extra credit at the end of the semester because of Iris's gift at bullshit. She was complicated... but she was amazing. She truly was."

Sofia was in tears as she finished the anecdote, half laughing and half crying, her grief for her friend palpable. It was so contagious that Carlee couldn't help but smile along.

Sensing the interview was ending, she stood up. "I promise you, Sofia, I'm going to do everything I can to find out who killed your friends. And I'm going to make sure they never lay a finger on anyone else."

Sofia nodded and wiped a lingering tear from her eye. "Vinny. I'm sure it was Vinny Garrard."

As they walked the few steps to her front door, Carlee spotted the letter that had been dropped through the mail slot at the beginning of their chat. Sofia bent down and picked it up, flipping it over to read the return address. Her brows immediately wrinkled.

"What the fuck?" Sofia breathed as a whole host of emotions fought for facial real estate—confusion, shock, worry—before she turned the letter over so Carlee could see the name scrawled across the front in a flourishing cursive. "I, um... I think this is for you?"

A spike of dread pierced Carlee's chest. It was only by the narrowest of margins and a small voice telling her to keep it together that she maintained even a mote of professionalism. Still, her wrist trembled as she reached out and plucked it from Sofia's hand.

Maybe this isn't what you think it is, the voice in the back of her mind proffered, but it sounded doubtful.

"Ah, right." She smiled at Sofia and peeked out the door to make sure the hallway was clear. "My partner was supposed to drop something important off for me." The lie sounded weak, even to her, and it didn't do much to ease Sofia's concern. "Sorry if it spooked you a little."

"I guess that's okay. If it's just your partner," Sofia said, thoroughly unconvinced, but apparently willing to go along for the sake of her own tattered nerves. Carlee made a mental note to ask Zack about parking a squad car outside her apartment for the next few nights, just in case. Whoever was leaving Carlee these threats had been following her, and she hadn't a clue as to their identity.

Knowing she couldn't read the note in front of Sofia, Carlee stepped out of the apartment and waved goodbye as confidently as she could muster. She headed for the elevator, her trembling hands tearing open the envelope a little more with each step.

The letter shook as she slid it out, and the red typeset filled her vision. She wanted to scream.

Making more money off the Eighth-Grade Killer's work, huh? You're a sick bitch, Carlee Knight, and no one would miss you if you disappeared. No one WILL miss you WHEN you disappear!

Chapter Twenty-Two

Lula Alford's condo building was shaped like a wizard's tower stuck in the wrong century. The facade had an old, retro feel to it, but Carlee couldn't put her finger on the style. Nor could she identify the massive abstract mural plastered across a good portion of it—beyond the fact it was supposed to be a jazz band playing at a club.

She went to the ancient call box by the front door, found *L. Alford*, and pressed the button. It rang twice.

"Hello?" Lula's voice peppered through, sounding distorted and far away. Apparently, it wasn't just the facade that was old-school in this place.

"Hi, Lula?" Carlee tried to put a smile in her voice, though after receiving the threat at Sofia's apartment a few hours earlier, it was difficult. "It's me, Carlee. I'm here."

"Just a moment, sweetheart," Lula said, and the door buzzed.

After visiting Sofia, Carlee had met with Zack to get the rundown of what he'd found at Aphrodite. While he was busy checking with his CPD contacts if Vinny had been questioned yet—and if he had, what he told police—Carlee charged herself with finding out as much about the victims as she could. They had to be connected in some way beyond attending Aphrodite, and Lula seemed to be her best bet at getting an unbiased opinion.

When Carlee arrived at her condo unit, Lula was already waiting at the door with a warm smile. "Come in, come in!" She puttered off toward the kitchen, leaving Carlee to wander into the living room. "I have a kettle on, so I hope you like black tea."

It was a stylish place—clean lines and fancy furniture, like the set of an old movie. Pop art prints hung on the walls, broken up by plaques and other awards Lula had earned throughout her career.

In the living room, Carlee found a wall full of pictures of Lula with various well-dressed, handsome people. One caught her eye.

"This isn't who I think this is, is it?" Carlee asked, leaning in to get a better look at the smiling man who had his arm around a younger Lula.

Lula carefully shuffled in with a tea set on a tray. "Yes, it is," she said, beaming at the memory.

"Are you serious? This is you with Donald Demonte? My dad loves his movies," Carlee gushed. It never hurt to butter up a potential source of information, but she was genuinely impressed.

"Your dad has good taste," Lula said, her voice awash with nostalgia. She placed the set on the coffee table. "That was at the premiere of *Twelve Days and Counting*. They don't make stars like Donald anymore..."

"I had no idea you worked on films." Carlee stood back and took in the whole tableau of photos, star after star of the art world, and let out a low whistle. "I hope Aphrodite knows how much they lucked out with you."

"You would think," Lula said, her smile stiffening a fraction. "I'm proud of all those pictures, but I'm even prouder of the ones over here." She nodded to a bookshelf filled with more photos.

"What are these?" Carlee asked.

"These are the ones I took with my star pupils… the ones I knew would be big one day."

Carlee stepped closer for a better look. Each photo featured a young up-and-comer with a bursting smile and their arms thrown around Lula in various exuberant, adoring poses.

"But I know you didn't come here to reminisce about the glory days," Lula said before ushering Carlee toward the sofa, her tone taking a stiff turn toward seriousness. "I figured you'd come by to talk to me after I heard about poor Yolanda Bradley."

"News travels fast around Aphrodite, huh?"

"I'm afraid so."

Now that she had Lula's permission, Carlee could dive right into the interview without further warm-up. "Did you know Yolanda personally?"

Lula sighed, busying herself with pouring tea. "Not very well. How do you take your tea, dear?"

"Straight, no sugar," Carlee said and accepted the cup. "To be honest, I wanted to stop by because I've run into a snag in my investigation, Lula."

"Oh?"

"Yeah. I was hoping you could give me some insight on the victims, the school, and the makeup industry as a whole."

"And you think I can help you with that?"

Carlee nodded. "You never know what seemingly tiny detail can blow open a stuck case."

"I'll tell you everything I know, of course," Lula said quickly, frowning as she poured herself a cup. "I'm just worried it might not be enough."

"I was under the impression you know the place inside and out," Carlee said. She took a sip of the tea. Though she preferred coffee, the hoity-toity brand Lula drank wasn't half bad.

"I did once, but I'm not sure how tuned in I am to the wheeling and dealing going on at Aphrodite at the moment."

"Why not?"

"Because I'm recently *retired* from my tenure there," Lula said, a hard edge creeping into her voice. She rolled her eyes and sighed again. "'Budget cuts,' you understand."

Carlee nearly choked on her tea. "You're kidding. Who in their right mind would let you go?"

"They'd rather get a cheap young thing to teach part-time, I'm sure." Lula held up her hands, a bitter wrinkle creasing her brow. "But I'll try to be as helpful as I can. Speaking of which..." She took a sip of tea and forced a brilliant smile. "How did your meeting with Jasmina go?"

"It... Um..."

"You're sitting in front of me, so it couldn't have gone too poorly."

Carlee fought against the swelling urge to spit out her mouthful of tea. Here it was—the conversation she'd been dreading. The one that had almost stopped her from making this call, let alone dropping by with another bucketload of questions. "Jasmina didn't... mention anything to you about it?" she asked carefully.

"Not a peep." Lula pursed her lips. "I haven't heard from her at all."

"Huh. Well, that's... odd," Carlee lied, trying not to gulp too suspiciously. She struggled to decide which was preferable: telling the truth and endangering her access to a potential source, or lying through her teeth. Lying won out. "It went well. As well as can be expected with the Duchess, anyway."

"Oh, what a relief," Lula said, her smile still beaming. Carlee pushed the disappointment she felt in herself down deep. "Did you get the answers you wanted from her?"

"Jasmina gave me some interesting information, that's for sure." Carlee blinked hard, working past the awkwardness of her dishonesty. "Though I was wondering if you could tell me anything about one of your coworkers—*former* coworkers," she corrected herself, wincing. "Vinny Garrard."

"Vinny? He's a wonderful colleague and a gifted artist," Lula said, her face lighting up. "He's an absolute joy to work with... and a total makeup nerd."

Carlee grinned, hoping Lula wouldn't bristle at a joke—and that the humor would steer her to a real answer. "Aren't you all makeup nerds at the heart of it?"

"Vinny and I are two wildly different species of nerd. Makeup is a very technical thing when you get into the nitty-gritty of it."

"From what I hear, Vinny is very into the nitty-gritty," Carlee said.

"Oh, you can say that again! He's been all over the world consulting with companies about their products. And have you been to his salon?"

Carlee sipped her tea, tiptoeing around the crux of her visit. "Not yet, unfortunately. But I've read some reviews, and it sounds amazing!"

"It certainly is. Though I'm not entirely sure why we're talking about Vinny Garrard."

"Well, I brought him up because I understand you're not alone in having trouble at Aphrodite..."

"What does that mean?" Lula sounded a little defensive.

"I'm not sure. Something about a contest gone bad last year?"

"Oh," Lula said, huffing crossly at the memory of it. "You have to understand, Carlee, that even for people as successful as Vinny and me, that contest was a big deal. The industry is far too obsessed with what an artist has done *lately*. I tried to tell Vinny that it was all just a game to Iris and her friends—that it was funny to them, not something to take so seriously—but it doesn't change the fact of the matter. Their catty fun took bread off their teachers' tables. Of *course* he was a little angry."

"I heard he was a lot more than a *little* angry," Carlee probed, remembering Sofia's terrified text messages.

"He might've overreacted a bit at first, it's true," Lula conceded. "But can you blame him? As her mentor, I was ashamed to hear Iris had any part in that horrible hazing campaign. But I know Vinny. He was laughing about it a few days later."

"It's just—"

"Look, I'll stop you right there, Carlee," Lula said. "Yes, he got mad at those girls. Hell, he wasn't the only one! But you came here to ask me about Vinny, so believe me when I tell you he was *certainly* not mad enough to hurt them. He doesn't have that kind of ugliness in his heart, I assure you."

"I'll take your word for it, then." Carlee took a deep breath and hoped Zack was making more headway. Lula wasn't going to give her anything on Vinny Garrard, much less a smoking gun. "Can you tell me anything more about Iris or the other girls?"

"I don't have much to add about my poor Iris," Lula said. She tutted into her teacup. "And regrettably, I never had the fortune of teaching Yolanda or Janie. I knew *of* them, of course, but I didn't really know them."

"I understand," Carlee said, sitting back in her chair. "You can't be expected to keep track of every student on campus."

Lula cradled her cup in her elegant hands as if to warm them. "They seemed like wonderful girls, mind you. I heard Janie, in particular, had quite the future ahead of her. She had some online thing that was getting to be very popular if I remember correctly."

"She was hoping to be a media influencer," Carlee said. Lula shook her head in what appeared to be exasperation at the new lingo. "Any chance you know Sofia Rollins, then?"

"Not beyond seeing her around the school," Lula murmured, biting her lip. "Why?"

"She was a friend of Iris's."

"Oh. I'm sorry I'm so useless to you, though I'd rather disappoint than embellish."

Carlee took a long, deep drink of tea to hide the surprise on her face. Sofia specifically mentioned being in Lula's class. Could one or the other have misremembered?

"Though now that you mention it," Lula said suddenly, raising a finger to cut Carlee's next question to the quick. "I do recall something you might find interesting."

Carlee perked up, intrigued. "Well, please, do tell."

"Not too long before she died and not too long before my forced retirement," Lula said, "Iris came into my classroom crying."

"About what?"

"She had been in some terrible fight with a friend of hers." Lula sighed. "She was so torn up about it that her waterproof mascara was running all down her face. I remember it clearly."

"Did she say what the fight was about?" Carlee asked, an eyebrow going up.

"She wouldn't tell me what it was about exactly—something about a lie or a nasty rumor or something—but I got the sense that it was deeply serious. She actually looked afraid."

"Did you know the person she was fighting with?"

"No, but it seems that *you* do," Lula said. She leaned closer toward Carlee, and Carlee unconsciously mirrored her. "It was Sofia."

Chapter Twenty-Three

Carlee Knight had no business being in a neighborhood like this—hell, she couldn't afford it. In her mind, the Gold Coast was the type of place that preferred *shoppes* instead of *shops*, and *wells* instead of *bars*.

"You want to stop and grab a coffee real quick?" Zack asked from the passenger seat. Carlee took her eyes off the road long enough to see he was pointing at a storefront.

She could tell he was only asking because Zack saw she was still shaken up about the threat at Sofia's place. Coffee was something he knew—or at least thought he knew—might comfort her. It was actually kind of sweet of him, but his tone would change when they walked in and he saw the prices.

"You think they do actual coffee?" she asked, trying her hardest to keep her eyes on the road rather than on her partner. "Or do you think they only do frou-frou stuff?"

"All I know," Zack said, "is that we'd probably have to take on a second gig if we wanted to make that our go-to meeting place."

"I'd say. It looks like Vinny Garrard operates at a different level than schmucks like you and me."

They were on their way to visit Vinny at his salon and ask him some tough questions. From what Zack's cop buddies could tell him, Vinny had alibis for each of the murders, but they were all from friends—and thereby struck Carlee as flimsy.

"You don't think this is a waste of our time, right?" she asked, watching Zack shrug out of the corner of her eye. "From where the investigation stands now, our main suspects are Sofia and Vinny. Sofia admitted to a rocky relationship with Iris, and I could hear the envy in her voice when we spoke. And Iris and Yolanda both bashed their teachers in that contest, which points to Vinny. But I still don't know how Janie plays into it, or why either of them would copy the Two-Faced Killer."

"I guess that means we're at the 'throw darts at the board' portion of our investigation," Zack said. "Everything I've seen still makes me think it's just some fucking loser who's upset no one will sleep with him."

"I hear you, but I just can't see it." Carlee jiggled her leg, trying to distract herself from a torrent of doubts. She could see several potential theories, but none of them answered every question. "It just doesn't add up. These murders have all been so close together and the method is so consistent, I can't help but think it's the actual Two-Faced Killer. Or a very good copycat."

"A 'good' killer? That's a hell of a choice of words, Carlee."

"You know damn well what I mean," she griped, plowing ahead. "Veteran serial killers can manage to kill at that pace and not get caught, but a copycat wouldn't be experienced enough to scrub the crime scenes, and neither Sofia nor Vinny is old enough to be the original Two-Faced Killer."

"Look, sometimes when you hear hoofbeats, it's a zebra and not a horse," Zack said. "But this one has 'horse' written all over it. Some true crime-loving dipshit out there watched a Two-Faced Killer documentary and thought to himself, 'That's what those whores at the beauty school deserve,' and has been taking out every girl who's dared to tell him no."

"I don't know what to tell you. I just don't see it," Carlee said.

Zack snorted. "Well, of course *you* don't see it."

"What's that supposed to mean?"

"It means that you're hung up on your own theories."

Bullheaded, isn't he? Ian's voice asked quietly in her ear. She could almost see his Hollywood smile.

"I'm hung up on following the evidence, Zack," Carlee corrected him. "And nothing we've seen so far says there's some random man out there running around killing beauty school students."

"Except for the trail of beauty school students' bodies," he said. Then, "I've been doing this a little longer than you have, Carlee."

"Agree to disagree." She gripped the steering wheel a little tighter but otherwise let the slight slide.

"I'm serious, my gut is telling me our guy is some basement-dwelling, artificial cheese-snack-eating, video game-playing nerd."

Carlee hit him with the full force of her signature eye roll. "Here we go again. How often does your gut have to be wrong before you stop listening to it and start trusting hard evidence? Maybe it's not a gut feeling," she jeered. "Maybe it's indigestion."

"I'll let you know when my gut starts failing me," Zack seethed, his neck flushed. "I know the profile for a killer like this, and I've got him pinned."

"I don't know how to put this gently for you," Carlee said as she rolled her window up. "But your *profile* for this murderer fucking sucks."

Zack went silent for a moment before leveling a finger at her. "Listen here, you—"

"Game face, West," Carlee said, cutting him off as she pulled up to the curb. "We're here."

The barely contained rage in Zack's face said it all—as if he needed reminding to put his "game face" on by some green PI like her. She couldn't help but smile, though she didn't find much pleasure in having the last word. Something big had shifted between them just now.

Maybe Ian *was* right. Maybe she shouldn't trust him.

A calming wave of lavender scent hit Carlee the moment they stepped into Vinny's salon. Every chair boasted plump, high-end leather upholstery, and the window glass was frosted to provide privacy from prying eyes. The products displayed at the front desk didn't list prices, but Carlee knew she could buy at least four bottles of her bargain-rack shampoo for one tiny tube of the conditioner this place sold.

"Come on in," Vinny called merrily, his footsteps echoing toward them from a room in the back. "Have a seat anywhere!"

His face was bright as ever when he stepped into the main room, but it dimmed when he saw Zack and Carlee standing there, probably confused by their unannounced visit—and the anger that still hung thick between them. "Oh. I didn't realize *you* two were dropping by. Is something wrong?"

"No," Zack said through gritted teeth. Then, with what Carlee could only imagine was great determination, he softened his voice. "We'd just like to ask you a few questions. Nothing more."

Vinny's smile wavered. "About the murders? Terrible business," he said. "I already spoke with some officers."

"We actually wanted to ask you a few more questions about your work and the industry in general," Carlee said, her reassurance easing Vinny's nerves a fraction. It was, of course, a bald-faced lie.

"Oh." Vinny's expression regained its strength. "Well, in that case, I'd be happy to chat."

"Place seems empty," Zack observed, nodding to the row of vacant chairs. "Times a bit lean in the salon business?"

"Hardly, Detective," Vinny said, his eyes narrowing but his smile unmoving. "My clients are what I would call 'late risers.' I open up early to get my ducks in order before they start trickling in."

"You see all these clients while you're still teaching at Aphrodite?" Zack pressed, stuffing his hands in his pockets, an attempt to appear casual and nonconfrontational as he grilled his target.

"Aphrodite aims to hire working professionals. To do that, they need to arrange courses with our schedules in mind, which usually means night classes. It works well since many of our students have day jobs too."

Carlee spotted her opportunity to step in. "Can you tell us a little more about your students?" she asked innocently. "I've been trying to get to know the victims and their friends."

"I might be able to help, but it depends who you're interested in."

"What about Sofia Rollins? Do you know her?"

Vinny gave a curt nod. "I do. She and Yolanda took my class together." A look of sudden dread overtook his chipper expression. "Oh my god. Has something... happened to her?"

"No, no. Sofia's fine. We're just trying to go through every possible avenue of investigation," Zack assured him, but Vinny's face never quite regained its full color. His worry seemed genuine to Carlee, but dread could stem from many sources—including the dread of being caught.

"I'm not sure I could tell you any more than I have already," Vinny said. "I didn't really know Iris or Janie at all."

"Are you sure?" Zack asked, his voice tightening as he shifted to the offensive.

Vinny's brows furrowed. "I don't understand the question. I didn't know them."

"Well, that's disappointing, Vinny. *Very* disappointing..."

"Why is that disappointing?"

"Because we heard that you did know Iris and that she royally screwed you in some competition," Zack explained. "Can you shed some light on that, Vinny?"

Vinny's face soured at the mention of the contest, but he either didn't pick up on Zack's hand-tailored suspicion or he decided to ignore it. "You heard right. She and Yolanda both had a good laugh at sinking their professors' chances of winning. Disgusting behavior from both... but I still can't say I really knew the girl."

"I don't blame you for getting worked up about it," Carlee jumped in, easily sliding into the Good Cop role. "I didn't see the screenshots, but from what I was told, those comments were downright bitchy. You went to administration?"

"I sure did," Vinny mumbled, "and it wasn't my proudest moment. Look, I know it might seem gauche to say, all things considered, but what they did was not worthy of Aphrodite. They were young, but they were certainly old enough to know they were in the wrong."

"Was Janie involved in that at all?" she asked.

"Not that I know of, but it wouldn't surprise me if she was."

"Why is that?" Carlee wondered out loud.

"From what I hear, she was making a name for herself by dragging every local makeup company through the mud on some web page or other."

"That actually fits with what I heard too," Carlee said, leading Vinny along. "You would think a young industry hopeful wouldn't go around burning every bridge they cross, right?"

"It was worse than burning bridges," he said gravely. "Had I pulled a stunt like that at their age, I would've been sent packing in a heartbeat with no hope of any future outside of a barbershop in Iowa."

Zack folded his arms. "Are you insinuating they didn't care?"

"Frankly? They didn't *need* to care, since there weren't any consequences," Vinny said, his feathers ruffling. A tinge of pink bloomed at his collar. "I don't often disagree with Aphrodite, but they needed to be taught a lesson, and it's a school's job to set examples for their students."

Taught a lesson. Carlee's fingernails bit into the flesh of her hand. She couldn't pounce yet, though. She'd bide her time, letting out the line before reeling in her fish.

"It must've hurt to lose that competition," she said.

"And getting that gig probably would've helped fill these seats," Zack added, once again nodding at the empty room. "Wouldn't it, Vinny?"

Vinny's face clouded as the nature of their questions became apparent to him. When he next spoke, it was with a straight back, a stern face, and clarity behind every word.

"Like I said before, my business is doing fine. I'm sure you can check my financials if you don't believe me. I might not have liked those girls, but I never wished harm on them. Not once."

Carlee shot a subtle glare Zack's way. "We're not accusing you of anything, Vinny. We're just trying to figure out the dynamics at Aphrodite."

"Right," he said sardonically. "And I'm sure you're here because everyone had great things to say about me."

"Actually, they did. You should know Lula Alford already vouched for you," Carlee said. She wondered if he thought as highly of her as she did of him.

"Ah, you talked to Lula," Vinny said like a sigh of relief, his entire body seeming to relax. "She's wonderful... one of the best teachers I ever worked with and a mentor to many."

"So I hear, but there's one thing that I just don't understand."

"What's that?" Vinny asked.

"If she's so wonderful, why did the school let her go? You'd think they could've found room in the budget to keep a teacher like Lula, even if it meant cutting the faculty party fund or whatever."

Zack narrowed his eyes at her as she finished the question. Carlee hadn't seen any reason to mention Lula's "retirement"—or, rather, layoff—on the ride here.

"Found room in the budget?" Vinny tilted his head quizzically. "What do you mean?"

"It just seems like they could've worked the numbers and found a way to save her job..."

"You think Lula was let go because of budget cuts?" Vinny snorted, shaking his head.

"She wasn't?"

"Hell no! Lula was fired. A host of students complained that she was too outdated, 'failing to prepare them for the workforce' or rubbish like that. They drafted a petition and the administration caved. The bastards," he threw in, sniffing derisively for good measure. "It was shameful, all of it."

"Are you sure?" Carlee inquired.

"Absolutely!"

"Did Lula know this was going on?"

"Of course. She confided in me as it was happening. God, the poor thing. She was so sick with stress. I was worried she was going to have a heart attack."

Carlee's mind buzzed, trying to align what she'd just heard with what Lula had told her the day before. She tried to justify Lula's deception. Maybe she'd been embarrassed, or maybe she'd thought it wasn't relevant, but Carlee couldn't come up with a satisfying reason for her to have lied about the nature of her dismissal. Carlee was a professional investigator working a murder case—she wasn't in a position to judge anybody for being fired.

As Zack asked Vinny about the intricacies of the students' power at Aphrodite, Carlee wandered the maze of her thoughts, trying to snatch the trailing thread of truth. She was still trying to wrap her head around it when her phone vibrated.

Ian: "You're not going to believe this."

Carlee: "What now?"

Ian: "There's a new victim."

Carlee's heart bottomed out as she read. She shoved the feeling aside—there was no time to allow emotion to control her.

Carlee: "Shit. Dressed, made-up, and posed?"

Ian: "All of the above... and her throat's been slit."

Carlee: "God damn it. When does it stop?"

Ian: "The Two-Faced Killer isn't stopping. If anything, they're speeding up."

Carlee: "No kidding. Send me the details."

Ian: "She was found in her apartment. I'll send you the address, but I'm too busy to meet you there."

Carlee: "Do we have an ID on the body?"

Ian: "Yep. Her name is—*was*—Sofia Rollins."

And with that, Carlee's heart, already at the floor of her stomach, seemed to crash through into the basement of her gut and shatter.

Chapter Twenty-Four

It took them more than twenty-four hours to get into Sofia Rollins's apartment, and by the time they had, CSI had already been through everything with a fine-toothed comb. Carlee thought Zack might've been able to make some phone calls to get them access the day-of, but no dice. The best he could do was get his hands on a copy of the lead detective's report.

When she finally did get inside the apartment, what Carlee saw matched up with what she had read. Sofia's body had long since been removed, but CPD had preserved everything else, including the pool of dried blood in the center of the living room.

"No signs of forced entry," Carlee said, stepping through the same room she had been in days before. She tried not to imagine Sofia, who had whispered her story for fear of being overheard, sprawled across the floorboards with an ugly smile cut into her neck.

"There was an open window," Zack said, motioning to the window by—but not on—the fire escape. Carlee judged the distance and figured it wasn't implausible for someone to get from *point a* to *point b*.

"It was hot yesterday, so it wouldn't be unusual for her to have opened it herself. Especially not with how old this place is." Carlee walked to the front door and peered down the hall, noticing several delivery boxes by tenants' doors. "Her neighbors also said there were several package deliveries."

Carlee thought back to the letter she had received as the familiar, iron-like grip of guilt clutched at her from inside. She couldn't help but feel responsible—that she had brought this down on Sofia just by meeting with her.

Zack nodded. "The people who found her said the front door was unlocked, so it's possible the killer disguised themselves as a mail carrier and ambushed her that way."

"Or she knew her killer and opened the door for a friend," Carlee said, completing the natural chain of theories.

They went through everything in the apartment as thoroughly as they could, hoping—praying—to find something CSI missed. But there was nothing. Not even a shred of new evidence.

As they walked out of the apartment block, disappointed, the sky rumbled at them. Storm clouds had blown in, signaling that driving rain and lightning were not far off.

"Well, that was a complete and total bust," Carlee said as she and Zack stalked up the sidewalk, their shoulders hunched with apprehension.

"We did what we could, Carlee. Sometimes there's no trail to follow, and that's just how the cookie crumbles."

"To hell with that. Sofia Rollins was *butchered* yesterday—surrounded by her neighbors—and there is absolutely nothing new for us to go off. No one saw a thing? No one heard a thing? The killer waltzed in and waltzed out and left us nil, nothing, nada? It makes no goddamned sense!"

Carlee's chest tightened as the reality of the situation grew clearer. Her anxiety drove her to walk faster. The image of dried blood on the creaky hardwood was still fresh in her mind, pooled underneath Sofia like Janie's and Yolanda's had been. As Iris's surely would have been.

Matching her speed, Zack let out a long, slow breath, shaking his head. Carlee thought he was about to say something, but he just worked his jaw. Any residual annoyance she had with him washed away at the sheer scale of the mystery that lay before them.

"What's our next move?" Carlee asked. "The once dormant Two-Faced Killer is at four recent victims, and at the pace they're going, it'll be days—not months, not weeks, *days*—before there's a fifth."

"I know," Zack admitted, his gaze set at the mid-distance. "Though it doesn't sound like the guys at the Second Precinct have made any headway. I think they're as in the dark as we are."

There was an old, dilapidated picnic table not far from Sofia's building, and Carlee went to take a seat. The wood had rotted on the ends, but it gave her a chance to sit and think. A moment later, Zack joined her.

"If they haven't gotten any closer, then we have to work harder," Carlee said, her voice rough in her throat. "I'll be damned if I let there be a fifth victim on my watch."

"Agreed. What do you think we should do next?"

"I think we should talk to Lula again," Carlee said decisively.

"Lula? You think she's hiding something?"

"Well, yeah. The other day she said Sofia wasn't in her class and I think that was a lie. She also lied about why she was let go from Aphrodite."

"What do you think she's sitting on, then?"

"I don't know. Maybe there are some inner workings of the school she doesn't want us to know about for whatever reason, and it might push the case forward. All we need to do is push *her* a little first."

"I'm not sure about that." Zack squinted. "Could it be something more? Sure. But it's likely just a little white lie, and to be completely open with you, Carlee, I think Lula's a waste of time."

Carlee sighed and began tapping her fingers against the splintered wood. "Likely. But I need more than *likely*, Zack."

"I think we should focus on the school support staff," he said. "Janitors, IT guys, other tertiary men working at the school, and look for the ones who match my initial profile: woman-hating bastard."

"Again with this bullshit?" Carlee's fingers stopped tapping, and she fixed Zack with a withering glare. He didn't flinch. "I thought we moved past this."

"I'm not trying to shove it down your throat or anything," Zack said, though his reluctance was artificial—Carlee could tell. "But I *do* have *several* more years of experience working this sort of case, and I'm telling you how this one is likely to turn out."

"There's that damned word again," Carlee said, exasperation thick in her voice. "You think Lula is a waste of time? What the hell do you think your random incel theory is?"

"I think it's worth at least some of your respect, considering I've been at this job since you were still learning how to wipe your ass properly in college." Zack stabbed his finger into the table, his eyes burning. "I have weathered an entire career of investigating robberies, sexual assaults, murders, and every other terrible thing under the sun. And what have you got? Two, three years of tailing adulterers? You help your FBI buddy and me solve a couple of murders, and all of a sudden, you're Sherlock fucking Holmes?"

"For fuck's sake!" Carlee stood, teeth bared, slamming her hands down on the table. "Honestly, Zachary? For a guy who has worked this job for years, you are *exceptionally* bad at it."

"Where the hell do you get off saying something like that to me? You know nothing about me!"

"I know enough! Ian told me all about what kind of a detective you are," Carlee sneered. She watched the words hit Zack like a slap across the face. Confusion flickered in his eyes before it was replaced by cold fury. "I know about all of the infractions. How, days before we met, you almost ruined an investigation by bulldozing through protocol."

"Oh, is that right?" he asked, daring her to continue. She did.

"He told me how you manhandle square pegs into round holes if it means being right about a suspect." Days ago, she had been afraid to mention these concerns, but they flowed freely from her now. "And *nothing* I've seen has convinced me any of that is wrong. The way you bull your way through these investigations, I wouldn't be surprised if you let a killer get away because you messed with the evidence."

"Is that all?" Zack said, his nonchalance pissing her off more. She couldn't see his hands, but she could imagine they were white-knuckled under the table, balled into fists.

"No, Zack, that's not all. Do you mind explaining why we couldn't get into the crime scene yesterday? You said you didn't want to step on the lead detective's toes?"

"I didn't—"

She cut him off, steamrolling ahead. "But was it that you didn't *want* to step on their toes, or you *couldn't* step on their toes?" Carlee asked. "Because *I* think your boss will kick your ass to the curb if you fuck around again. I think she's as concerned as I am about you screwing with evidence."

"You don't know what you're talking about," Zack stammered. He stared her down, his face as dark a red as she had ever seen it. But it wasn't enough to deter her. She had started, and she was going to finish.

"What's worse is that I don't think you would even *try* to screw up the investigation. You just would." Carlee huffed, adrenaline coursing through her system.

Part of her knew she was crossing a line, the Rubicon, but another part of her knew this was necessary. She was going to have this conversation with him at some point, and it was better to do it now than after he had irrevocably screwed something up.

"It scares the hell out of me that you're going to do this with the Eighth-Grade Killer, and they're going to get away because of it. And I can't risk that, Zack. It's why I've been telling you to stop jumping to conclusions and why it pisses me off when you just keep doing it."

"You done yet? Was that the end of your tantrum?" Zack asked, rage sharpening his already icy voice. He didn't explode or scream like a kettle, which—to Carlee—made the whole situation that much worse. "I don't know if it was you or Garnett who had the bright idea to treat me like I'm some criminal, but fuck both of you. That smarmy, greasy FBI kid—I can at least understand him. But you? We've worked together, Carlee. You could've asked me about any of this at any time."

"I didn't think I needed to…"

"You had every chance to, but you didn't." Zack's lip curled, and the edge of his voice could've splintered the table between them. "We were supposed to be partners in this, Carlee."

"We're still partners, but—"

"No, we're not! You *don't* pull some bullshit like this on your partner! The fact you'd trust that walking, talking G-Man ad before you'd even talk to me tells me you don't know nearly as much as you think you do."

"That's—"

"That's enough." Zack cut her off one last time. "I let you say your piece and I've heard enough. The bottom line is that we have a serial killer on the loose, and you two thought it would be a great idea to waste your time investigating *me*."

They glared at each other across the table, chests heaving. The sky above crackled as the wind whipped around them.

"You know what? Fuck this." Finally, Zack stood up. He stepped away from the table and stormed toward his car.

"Where are you going?" Carlee asked. Part of her wanted to grab his arm and stop him. Part of her wanted to shove him along.

"Away," Zack said shortly. "This partnership isn't working. Never worked."

"Just hold on a—wait!"

"Fuck you. Do what you gotta do, but do it without me."

Carlee stood there on the sidewalk, watching Zack walk off. Mostly she wanted to scream every known obscenity and assure him that she'd be better off this way. Yet some part of her, deep down, was already melancholic that their work together was over.

There was a final crack above her, and the clouds released a torrent of rain. She soon lost track of Zack, the downpour obscuring his car as he drove away.

If that's how things had to play out, so be it.

She would finish this case—and all of her future cases—alone.

Chapter Twenty-Five

Carlee had done plenty of dumb things in her life of tech geekery and infidelity espionage. She even had the fresh scars to match.

Even so, every sensible voice in her head—Eleanor's, Ian's, Alicia's, even Zack's—was screaming at her that this thing was *particularly* dumb.

After her falling out with Zack, Carlee had come back to this wizard's tower of a condominium to confront Lula about her lies. Lies Lula had fed a private investigator while she was chasing the scent of an active serial murderer.

And now here she was, sitting in Lula's living room, with no partner.

Dumb or not, what was the worst thing that could happen? Carlee had tried her best not to answer that question after her calls had gone to Ian's voice mail for the fifth time.

She had, for a fraction of a second, considered calling Zack to see if he'd go with her, but frankly, she would rather eat dirt. Zack would've spent the entire interview leveling snide remarks at both her and Lula, and then complained on the way there and back about how she'd wasted their time. And that was assuming he would've spoken to her in the first place.

No. She would do this alone.

"It's so nice seeing you again, dear." Lula tutted, fanning herself with a hand. "You'll have to forgive me. You didn't let me know you were coming, or I'd have something prepared."

"Don't worry about it, Lula."

"Can I at least offer you some more tea?"

"That won't be necessary. This won't take long." The phantom taste of Lula's expensive black tea danced over her tongue. "I just have a few follow-up questions. I'll be out of your hair in no time."

"Oh, hush. I don't know about you, but I'm a host, and that requires at least the bare-minimum effort," Lula said, gently smiling. "So, what can I get you? Lemonade? A water?"

"You know what? Sure. Maybe a bottle of water for the road?" Carlee asked innocently enough. She wasn't sure what Lula was hiding—or if it was at all important to the case—but it was better to be safe than sorry, and Carlee wasn't about to get comfortable in the house of someone who had lied to her before. *Twice.*

"Of course." Lula was already moving to the kitchen, pleased to fulfill her hosting duties. "I have a few bottles in the fridge."

She returned holding two bottles of artisanal water, and Carlee gave her a gracious smile as she reached across the coffee table to accept one.

She cracked it open and took a few sips, if only to put Lula at ease. Her host had already taken several gulps from her own bottle and was sitting patiently, waiting for Carlee to finish drinking before they spoke in earnest.

"So, now that we're all settled," Lula began, sinking back in her seat, "to what do I owe the pleasure? Come to pick my brain about the industry again? I can only hope it's not to ask for another audience with the Duchess."

Lula was going above and beyond to play the good hostess, but her eyes had grown intense, her smile a little too wide. Carlee knew that to say Lula was annoyed with her would have been an understatement.

"About that," Carlee said. She bit her lip and tried to come up with the words. "That meeting... didn't quite go as planned."

Lula's smile flickered for the briefest of moments. "So I've heard."

"Did Jasmina call you?" Carlee asked, wincing at the fiasco her sting had become.

"Oh no, Jasmina won't be speaking with me for a good long while," Lula said shortly. "I had to find out through a mutual business acquaintance. Who also, coincidentally, won't be speaking to me for a good long while." She laughed lightly, the bottle in her hand crackling as her grip tightened.

"I cannot stress enough how sorry I am if I made things difficult for you. If there's anything I can *legally* do to—"

"Don't be silly. You were there on behalf of my students. I can't be upset about that," Lula said, waving off the offer, the tension draining out of her voice. "So I won't be on Jasmina's Christmas card list for a while. I'll live."

Carlee was quite sure she herself wouldn't make it on Lula's Christmas card list after the conversation they were about to have.

Every word Lula said was wrapped in warmth, her priorities all in the proper order... mostly. But now that Carlee was looking for it, she could glimpse a carefully crafted veneer draped over every action Lula took—the expert camouflage of the matriarchal instructor, cloaking a cutthroat professional accustomed to a lifetime of guarding her status. Had Carlee not caught onto the lies, she would've never seen through the ornamentation. It was her own brand of makeup, and it was just as potent as anything Aphrodite could teach.

Carlee sized up Lula one last time, calculating the best path for an interrogation attack. Lula seemed to be in control of herself—or at least thought she was in control of herself—and that would have to change. Carlee needed to unsettle her enough to trip the master pretense artist over her own lies.

And she knew an easy—if direct—way to do just that.

"I'll cut to the chase," Carlee said, leaning back in her seat and offering Lula a perfectly patient feline smile. "Why did you do it?"

She had expected any number of reactions—confusion or anger chief among them. She did *not* expect Lula to calmly remove the cap from her bottle and take a long sip, with an even larger smile plastered across her face, all while staring at Carlee, unblinking. A shiver ran down her spine as Lula casually replaced the cap. Alarms were blaring in her subconscious, but why?

"I was doing the industry a service," Lula said candidly.

"And by that, you mean...?" Carlee couldn't shake the feeling that she was a hapless cat who had chased a mouse into a pit viper's den, and now the snake blocked her exit.

"I mean I was doing the industry a service when I killed them, of course," Lula said.

The blood in Carlee's veins seemed to turn to water. Every cell of her body began to go stiff.

"That's what you're asking, isn't it? Why did I kill them?" Lula set the half-finished bottle on the table between them. The smile hadn't moved a millimeter. "It's as I told you, dear. I was doing the industry—the world, if we're being honest, but I tend to think that sounds too grandiose—a service."

It was like trying to move through a room full of sand. No matter how many liars she caught in the act—and these days, no matter how many murderers she crossed paths with—there was always an initial moment of realization, a bolt of horror, that stopped Carlee dead in the water. She couldn't move. The blunt force of the confession had turned her into stone.

Her thoughts were blank, and she struggled to find something to say.

"Why?" was all Carlee managed to get out.

"*You're* asking why? Carlee Knight, shouldn't you know already?" Lula asked, standing up and walking to the bookcase, where the photos of her students were arrayed. "They were poison. Murder isn't a pretty thing, believe me, but sometimes it's necessary. Unfortunately, to deal with the ugly elements of the industry, sometimes you must yourself become ugly."

Lula, her back turned, began to pick up and inspect the photos. Carlee couldn't see her face, but she got the feeling Lula was smiling.

"They were innocent," Carlee heard herself say. The fine hairs on her arms prickled, and she wanted to leap out of the chair, but the shock was holding her down. "You were their mentor. You were supposed to help them."

"They were no such thing!" Lula whirled around, her protest loud and piercing, her eyes wild and more viperous than ever before. "They would've *destroyed* the innocents, the artists just starting, just trying to make it."

"The only one they threatened to destroy was you!" Carlee shouted, her breath stuttering in her chest as she realized why her body felt so heavy.

There was only one reason Lula would tell Carlee any of this. She planned on silencing her. She wasn't even slightly worried that Carlee would expose her. And a part of Carlee—the part that felt like the task of standing up had suddenly become impossible—knew it was already too late to fight back.

"I'm sorry, but that's simply not true," Lula said calmly. She stepped closer, the snake uncoiling. "Because I *was* one of the innocent ones. When I started in this industry, everyone said I was too young, too inexperienced. The models were the worst. The things I would hear them say about me, the way I'd see them look at me... and all girls like me. Like we were trash. Less than human."

In the moments Lula studied her photographs, Carlee had slid her hand into her pocket, secretly fumbling for her phone. If she remembered correctly, the screen was still set on her recent call list, leaving only one feasible option—Zack. Zack might hate her, but he was enough of a professional to at least answer her call.

She mashed her finger into the lower half of the screen, hoping it would strike true and find his name.

"And so you started killing," Carlee said, praying that if she managed to call Zack and he answered, he would at least hear Lula's confession. "Is that when you became the Two-Faced Killer?"

"Such a garish name." Lula snickered, her lip curling. "I simply made their outside appearance match their inside appearance. The horrible clothes, the sloppy makeup, the poses—I was showing the world exactly what kind of people they were."

"But you stopped, Lula. Why? How?"

"Killing those girls wasn't some *compulsion*. What kind of a monster do you think I am?" Lula asked, confusion knitting her sculpted eyebrows. "I set out to send a message, and I sent it. When I started getting the jobs and respect I deserved, the models stopped trying to sabotage me. And that was the end of it. Everyone went on, and I enjoyed a successful career. Because of my spring cleaning, the industry grew for the better."

"And Janie?"

"Ah, Janie," Lula said, rolling her gaze up to the ceiling. "She was the one who opened my eyes to this new crop of monsters. Not models this time, not in this generation... but nasty, trash-talking critics. They needed to help teach their peers a lesson about respect."

"You killed them for *trash-talking*?"

Lula crossed the space between them in an instant, almost inhumanly quick. Carlee could do nothing but bare her teeth as Lula roughly grabbed her jaw, cold fingers digging deep into her cheeks.

"They were instigators of pain, Carlee. Ruining the futures of bright young people before they even had a chance... and we all deserve a chance. I thought you might understand, but you obviously don't." Lula released her face only to slap it.

Carlee struggled to refocus, but the world was spinning and her ears had begun to softly ring.

"That low-life piece of shit, Janie," Lula snarled, "got me fired from Aphrodite. Do you think I *needed* a job there? No, I took the teaching position to give back to the industry."

"You were... You were doing them a favor," Carlee muttered, her tongue woolly and stubborn. She had to keep Lula talking. "And Janie didn't recognize it?"

"She spat in my face," Lula went on, her eye beginning to twitch. "She called me a fossil. A relic of an ugly time. It made me furious, but I wasn't going to kill her for having stupid opinions. Not until she complained to Aphrodite that I wasn't 'preparing students for the industry.' Can you believe that? I *am* the industry! And so I did to her what I did to those monsters all those years ago. I left her body by the school as a warning."

"A warning they didn't hear," Carlee said, the faces of the three other victims flashing through her mind.

"Didn't hear it, didn't understand it—doesn't matter," Lula said, flipping her hand back and forth. "Iris and Yolanda each made their little comments, each trying to tear me down, and so they were my next lesson."

"And Sofia?" Carlee croaked. Squeezing her eyes shut against the throbbing in her skull, she hoped beyond hope that she wasn't about to have her fears confirmed.

"Yes, Sofia," Lula echoed, her smile growing even more vicious. "Sofia had her moments... and thought she knew more than she did. But I probably wouldn't have gone after her if you hadn't told me she was talking about me. Thanks for the heads up, by the way."

Carlee's body racked and her heart sundered. Tears began to well at the edges of her eyes and spill down her cheeks, but she didn't feel them.

Her heart, once hammering in her chest, now felt heavy. Slow.

"Oh no, dear, don't cry," Lula said, kneeling before Carlee. She wiped away the tears, cupping her cheeks in her hands. "You'll ruin your complexion."

Carlee couldn't speak anymore. She tried to reach up and grab Lula's arm, shove it away, but she found she couldn't move a muscle. The water bottle fell to the floor with a thud, and the sound resonated through her bones.

"I hope that by now, you've caught on to the little treat I slipped you." Lula whispered. The image of her began to shift and slide in Carlee's vision. The words—the whole world—sounded so far away.

She fought against the fog, but it enveloped her anyway.

"Just lie back and enjoy the ride," Lula cooed, and the last thing Carlee saw was her serpentine smile. "I'm sure this is your first time experiencing ketamine."

Chapter Twenty-Six

The next time Carlee stirred, the world was white. Everything that was and ever had been was a bright, gleaming white. Hot, pure, and unending.

"How long have I been here?" Carlee asked. Her jaw refused to move, but somehow it felt like words were still escaping her.

Forever, a voice said. *And you will be here forever.*

No, not quite, another voice chimed in. *There was something before this, but I can't quite remember what it was. It was so long ago.*

Forever ago, said the first.

With great effort, Carlee tried to concentrate. Moments felt like eons, but eventually, she brought the voices into focus. She almost thought she recognized them...

"Cameron?" she called into the whiteness, struggling to find him in the fog. "Cameron, are you there?"

Does everything have to be about Cameron with you? the first voice scoffed. *You're close, Carlee, but no cigar.*

We're your thoughts, said the second voice. *In case you couldn't tell.*

You're dying, Carlee, said the first voice. *You need to wake up. Fight back!*

She pushed herself harder, but her limbs had turned to stone. The white void that stretched in front of her cleared, and she could only make out a shadow, swinging and swinging—the blade of a fan.

She was looking at the ceiling. Slowly, frame by frame, a face slid into her view, and through the nebulous fog, she remembered where she had seen the face before. It was Lula Alford.

The voices in her head began to shout and wail and gnash their teeth, but Carlee couldn't understand them anymore. It was as if Lula Alford's face had pushed them far away.

"Oh, good. You're awake," Lula said soothingly. "I was worried you wouldn't be joining me for these final moments."

"What's going on?" Carlee asked.

"You don't need to worry, dear. I'll take care of everything." Lula's laughter bounced around the room.

She reached out and gently grabbed Carlee's chin. Or rather, what had once been her chin—she wasn't sure if it was hers anymore or even that it *was* a chin. Lula began swaying her face from one side to the other.

"You know, I've never even tried ketamine, but I'm told it's quite pleasant." Lula's voice was a cushion, soft and supportive. She began moving something even softer back and forth across Carlee's cheek. It might have been a brush, and it felt wonderful. "You can't move, your breathing slows, and things just... slide around a bit. An out-of-body experience, if you will."

Carlee, too, began to slide. She slid until she was somehow outside herself, looking down. She saw Lula standing over her, applying makeup. She saw herself sitting on the couch, her head tilted up, resting on a pillow. It was such a serene scene that she almost wanted to cry.

"No, no," Lula said, lightly slapping her cheek, causing Carlee to crash back into herself. "Stay with me as much as you can, dear. You need to hear this."

"Hear what?" Carlee murmured, but Lula made no indication that she heard her.

"I need you to know that I'm sorry," Lula said, frowning. "I dealt with those hideous girls because the world is better off without them, but you haven't done anything wrong. As far as I can tell, you're just as beautiful on the inside as you are on the out. But you pried open things that should've stayed shut. Tried to help people who shouldn't be helped."

"What are you..." Carlee struggled to talk, but it was like trying to fit pieces from a hundred different puzzles together. "What are you saying?"

Lula tutted. "Oh, sweetheart, I know you think you're talking, but all you're doing is groaning. If you want to know how all this happened to you, it was the bottle of water. Asking for a bottle instead of just a glass? Dead giveaway you were onto me." She sighed airily and tweaked Carlee's nose. "As for how I got the ketamine in—a sharp syringe and a little applied heat, and the bottle was as good as new."

The damned bottle! the first voice shouted, breaking into Carlee's consciousness. *We'll have to remember that for next time.*

Awfully optimistic, aren't we, the second voice said thinly. *There won't be a next time.*

Lula began to hum to herself as she applied another dusting of makeup to Carlee's face. "Don't worry," she cooed. "I'm not making you up into some cartoon whore like the others. You don't deserve that. You'll get a classic look, a beautiful dress, and a dignified pose.

Maybe I'll have you pondering with a finger on your lips... I think your right side is the best, so I'll have your head turned slightly up and to the left like you're deep in thought. Yes, that'll be just lovely. Picture perfect. And before you ask—no, the slash won't hurt a mite."

We're running out of time, the first voice said.

Carlee, cried the second voice, *don't listen to her. You need to listen to us!*

The voices were closer now, sharper. They sounded familiar, and Carlee strained to hear them more clearly. She felt that it was of supreme importance to find them. To talk to them. If only she could move. If only she could just turn her head.

"Beautiful," Lula said. "It won't be long now." She leaned over to look down into Carlee's eyes, smiled so gently, and then went back to work.

Carlee tried to fight, tried to move, tried to do anything, but it was useless. She screamed, but no one seemed to hear her.

You need to understand this, Carlee, the first voice said.

And then, together, they started to shriek it:

This is all your fault.

Chapter Twenty-Seven

The tires squealed, and rubber burned as Zack's car slid to a stop outside Lula Alford's condo. He had already called in backup, but there was no telling when they'd make it. Not fast enough.

He pulled the key and jumped out, racing toward the front door. His shotgun and vest were in the trunk, but based on what he'd heard on the phone, he had no time to gear up.

Zack swore under his breath as he barreled past someone exiting the front door, hoping against hope that he wasn't already too late.

The phone call replayed over and over in his mind: Carlee's increasingly slurred words running alongside Lula's confession, then a detailed description of how she would dispatch Carlee. He had been dead silent as he listened, worried that if Lula heard him—if the Two-Faced Killer heard him—she'd know Carlee had managed to place a call, and she'd kill her before he could so much as blink.

So he had raced to his car, able to think about nothing but a knife pressed against Carlee's throat. Nothing else except the last thing he said to her.

Do what you gotta do, but do it without me.

His head whipped left and right, looking for the stairwell. He found the door by the elevator and sprinted to it.

If she's dead, it's my fault, he thought, struggling to keep moving through the hurricane of doubts. *If she's hurt, it's my fault. Carlee attracts trouble like flies, and I walked away and let it happen.*

He'd been so angry with her, so deeply betrayed by her mistrust. Even now, he wasn't sure why he had seen her incoming call and hit the green button instead of the red, but he thanked his lucky stars he did.

His legs pumped, his hamstrings searing as he bounded up the steps, trying to stay focused, trying not to think of the myriad ways he had fucked up. How he should've checked on Carlee sooner. How, if he had just kept his cool, she wouldn't have gone there without him.

Marisol had ripped him a new asshole not three days ago in front of all his colleagues and peers, and it hadn't bothered him nearly as much. Why had Carlee gotten under his skin the way she had?

Maybe it was because she was right. Not just about him, but about the case. And now she might die for it, just because he wouldn't bend, not even an inch.

He was out of time to think. Lula's door stood before him like a portal to a hell he wasn't ready to enter. Every part of him screamed to destroy it, to kick it open and get it all over with, but something about that hallway slowed him down. It was quiet, almost eerily so. Instead of crashing around like a bull, he laid his ear against the door, straining to make sense of the muffled voice inside.

"Wait here for a moment," he heard Lula say. Her voice was close, but then her footsteps padded away, heading somewhere deeper into the condo, away from the entrance. When she spoke again, it was a soft call, muffled by distance. "I'll be right back to finish up, dear."

It could only mean one thing: Carlee was still alive—if only just barely, if only just for the moment. But that was all he needed. If Carlee was still breathing, he would move heaven and earth to make sure she stayed that way. He sure as hell could move this damned door.

Zack leaned back and planted his foot—along with all of his weight—right above the knob, sending it flying open. His gun was out and ready. He had prepared himself for the possibility of sweeping the home door-by-door, room-by-room, but Carlee was right there in front of him. She was sprawled on the couch, her black t-shirt and jeans a stark contrast to the primarily white living room.

"Holy shit!" Zack gasped as he rushed to her. Lula was nowhere in sight. He placed his gun on the floor beside his knee, using both hands to gently move Carlee's head and pry her eyelids open. "Carlee, speak to me. Say something—anything you want. Call me a fucking idiot. Just one word."

He'd arrived in time to stop her throat from being slashed, but there was still the possibility that Lula had overdosed her. Only Iris had survived the initial drugging, and that was solely thanks to a rare medical condition. He fumbled ineptly for a pulse, his hand shaking too badly to find it right away.

"Hmm..." Carlee's eyes rolled back into her head. She was breathing—barely.

The sound of feet rushed toward the living room. There wasn't time to perform a thorough checkup or to move her. He reached for his gun, whipped around, and lifted it right as Lula Alford turned the corner at a dead sprint, wielding a kitchen knife.

She stumbled to a stop at the sight of the barrel pointed directly at her, but she didn't cower. On the contrary, she seemed far too relaxed at the wrong end of a gun.

"How'd you find out?" she asked coolly.

Zack instinctively twitched. His aim didn't falter and his eyes didn't leave her, but his body flinched toward Carlee.

Understanding burned in Lula's stare. "Ah, I see. She's far too clever."

"Drop the knife!" he barked with all the authority that a decade of service with the Chicago Police Department gave him. "Lula Alford, you are under arrest. Drop the knife and back away!"

It was a voice hard enough to put seasoned gang captains in their place, but it didn't make Lula Alford do a damned thing. All she did was peer at Zack, calculating. He could see her grip on the knife tighten as she did the math, counting the steps that stood between it and his chest.

Carlee was right. She was the Two-Faced Killer, responsible for untold bloodshed. But there in that living room, even holding a knife, she was also a woman in her late fifties. Would he hesitate to shoot? Even a moment, even a millisecond, might mean Carlee's death.

He heard more than saw Lula's foot slide back, position itself to give her dash a faster start. Without even noticing it, his finger began to squeeze the trigger. He had put thousands of rounds down the firing range—even used his gun in the line of duty several times—and knew exactly how many pounds of pressure it would take to fire the weapon and end this woman's life. He was about halfway there when he paused.

The sirens outside surprised them both, and for the briefest of moments, Zack worried Lula would charge. Something seemed to change in her, though. Maybe she realized it was over, that there was no escape. Maybe she was just tired and the full weight of her actions had finally begun to drag on her. Whatever the reason, she straightened up and slowly lowered, then dropped the knife. With a solid *thunk*, it sliced through the carpet and dug deep into the floor.

Relief flooded him, cool but sludgy. He felt in his gut that she wouldn't try to attack him now, but his gut had been entirely wrong about her before—perhaps deathly so. His pistol remained leveled directly at her heart.

They stood there for a few moments that felt like forever until backup finally stormed through the open front door.

Just before they handcuffed and dragged her away, Lula cast a gaze at Zack that terrified him with its sincerity. "I'm really sorry it had to be this way," she said. "She was one of the good ones. I don't expect her to survive, and I'm so sorry for your loss."

The calmness in her voice nearly sent Zack into a panic, every hair on his body standing on end. The Two-Faced Killer must've known she wouldn't be able to hurt anyone else now—unless she already knew she had.

Zack whipped around and rushed to Carlee, still motionless on the couch, her eyes half closed. He crashed to his knees and searched again for a pulse in her throat. He found a faint beat of life, but it was growing fainter.

"We need an ambulance!" Zack yelled at the uniforms behind him, praying they wouldn't be too late. "Somebody get her a fucking ambulance!"

He turned back to Carlee's limp form and tried to open her eyes, but there wasn't any response.

"Stay with me, Carlee," Zack whispered to her, hoping she could hear him, hoping he was getting through. "Just a little longer and help will be here. Please just stay alive."

He grabbed her hand. It wouldn't do anything, but he couldn't do much else.

All of a sudden, her body started to shake and convulse. He cried out in surprise, not knowing what to do, and the rest of the world disappeared as Zack West tried through sheer will to keep Carlee Knight from falling off the precipice.

Chapter Twenty-Eight

Carlee Knight was getting tired of hospitals. Scratch that. She was getting *sick* and tired of hospitals.

Giggling—out loud—at her own pun didn't help the matter one bit. The only thing that kept her from falling into complete madness was that Alicia had taken time off work to keep her company.

"What're you thinking?" Alicia asked, a forkful of the chocolate pecan pie she had smuggled in for them to share hovering in front of her mouth. "You've got that look on your face you get when you think of a really funny joke."

"Nothing," Carlee said. She stuffed a bite of pie into her mouth to dissuade further questions.

She had only been there for about twelve hours and would only be there until the doctor was sure the ketamine had worked its way through her system—in case she suffered some sort of delayed reaction to the drug—but it still felt like forever. The fact she had practically lived in hospitals for the past couple of months wasn't exactly helping.

Carlee had almost called Eleanor and asked her to bring a drone by so she could at least tinker—maybe even take one to the children's ward, knowing how much kids liked them—but she wasn't ready for the "I told you so" lecture she was positive she was going to get. This one was sure to be a doozy.

The only thing that could make this already bad situation worse would be if her father somehow got wind of her condition and stormed into the hospital. With every passing moment, that possibility inched closer to reality. Carlee impatiently looked at the door, willing someone with the authority to release her to walk in.

There was a crisp, strong knock.

"Oh, shit," Alicia said around the fork in her mouth. She desperately grabbed the pie container off Carlee's bedside table and was futilely looking for a place to hide it when Zack popped the door open and tentatively stepped in.

"Hey. Are you up?" Zack asked sheepishly, making a show of looking up at the ceiling and behind the door, as if he had somehow missed her flopped in the uncomfortable hospital bed.

"No. I'm down here," Carlee said, icily mocking his tone. He grimaced a little, and she immediately regretted it. The last time she had seen him—remembered seeing him, at least—they had parted on poor terms, but a lot had happened since then.

"You're Zack, right?" Alicia glanced at Carlee, eyebrows raised quizzically.

"I am, yeah."

"It's so nice to meet you!" She shot out of her chair to shake Zack's hand vigorously, which seemed to confuse him more than anything. "I'm Alicia! Carlee told me so much about you."

"She's exaggerating," Carlee added. She decidedly *hadn't* told Alicia about the falling out, or she would've been much cooler toward him.

"Whatever, Carlee," Alicia giggled, then turned to Zack again. "By the way, you scared the hell out of me just now."

"Me? Why?" he wondered.

"I thought I was going to go to hospital jail or something for sneaking in this pie."

Zack scrunched his brow. "Unless she's on a restricted diet, I'm pretty sure you're allowed to bring pie into the hospital."

"Really?" Alicia seemed to deflate at the news. "Well, that fun fact took the fun right out of sneaking food in here, didn't it?"

Zack shook his head, seemingly baffled by Alicia's relentless happiness and non sequiturs. Then he looked back at Carlee, his gaze dipping again, and she was stunned to witness Zack West look... *shy*?

"Do you remember what happened?" he asked.

"Sort of," Carlee said after a moment. "I drifted in and out. I do know you saved my ass, even though I don't really remember it."

Zack exhaled, and Carlee girded herself. She wasn't in the place—mentally or physically—to deal with scolding or gloating, but if anyone had earned the right to give her a lecture, it was him.

"It was foolish to go talk to Lula by yourself. Especially if you thought she was dangerous. Are you that stupid?" he demanded sternly.

"You told me to go at it alone, so..."

"I told you to go at it without *me*, and I admit that was a mistake, but why didn't you at least ask Garnett to back you up? Or anybody?"

"I like him already," Alicia said from Carlee's side, holding her fingers up like she was trying to draw a waiter's attention. "I was waiting for someone who'd be fierce enough to scold you for scaring us to death like that."

Carlee looked back and forth between her best friend and her sort-of-partner and couldn't help but feel ganged up on. She was the one in the hospital bed, wasn't she? Shouldn't they give her a bit of a break?

"If I was absolutely positive that Lula was the Two-Faced Killer, I would've asked for backup," Carlee protested, trying not to squawk at the hard looks Alicia and Zack were leveling at her. "All I knew was that she lied to me. It made her suspicious, sure, but not in an 'is she going to drug me and slit my throat?' kind of way. All I wanted was to ask her a few questions and see if she'd slip on something useful."

"Was it the tea?" Zack asked.

"No. It was a *sealed* water bottle. I squeezed it before I drank it—the security ring cracked when I took the cap off! I thought it was safe."

"You're lucky you're alive." Zack frowned at her, taking a few steps closer to the bed. "And you're lucky you had the presence of mind to call me so I could record Lula's confession before you were paralyzed. I just wish you would have reached out *before* you waltzed into her lair," he said gruffly.

"Yeah, well, I hate to be the one to bring it up, but you were furious with me at the time."

"I answered your call, didn't I?"

"Honestly? I wasn't sure if you would. I thought you never wanted to work with me again," Carlee reminded him. She spotted Alicia watching, her cup and straw positioned in such a way that she looked engrossed in the latest episode of *Chicago Wives Unchained*. She was lucky Zack was there, or Carlee would've thrown something at her.

"Bullshit, Carlee. You called because you know that it doesn't matter how mad I am at you," he insisted, his face glum. "I will always help if my help is needed."

"See... Ian was right about you," she said, nodding.

"What did that snake..." Zack stiffened, his shoulders hunching as if preparing himself to be raked across the coals. It was a look with which he appeared to have much practice, but despite it, he calmly added, "What about?"

Carlee grinned at him. "When you say shit like 'I will always help if my help is needed,' you really *do* sound like Officer Friendly."

Alicia tried not to laugh, forcing herself to cough instead as Zack's stiffness melted into an eye roll.

Sure enough—and speak of the devil—there was another knock at the door. Carlee could tell from the impatient pop of the knuckles it wasn't a nurse with discharge papers.

"Carlee Knight, am I going to have to..." Ian stopped midstep as he spotted Zack and Alicia surrounding Carlee's bed, leaving the door swinging shut behind him. "Oh, hey, everyone," he uttered, holding a modest *Get Well Soon* bouquet that drooped in his hand.

Carlee could've sworn she saw his million-dollar smile flicker.

"Nice to see you too, Garnett," Carlee said, adjusting to the sudden coolness in the room. She wondered if Alicia had picked up on the spike in tension. "You know Zack, and this is my friend, Alicia. Alicia, I am only somewhat dismayed to introduce Special Agent Ian Garnett."

Something changed in his smile. It couldn't have shifted more than a fraction—more than a fraction of a fraction—but Carlee swore it became even more dazzling as Alicia returned it. Carlee wondered if they had a personality class at Quantico—approximately two seconds after she wondered if Ian Garnett was aware of how hard she would hit him if he turned his Hollywood charms on her best friend.

"It's a pleasure to meet you, Alicia," Ian said, holding his wobbling lilies aside with one hand to shake hers with the other. "If Carlee decides to get herself into any more trouble, please give me a call." Out of nowhere, like a practiced close-up magician, he produced a business card and handed it to Alicia, who was apparently too taken aback by all the theatrics to do much more than nod her head dumbly.

Carlee wished Alicia was near enough to pinch.

"Garnett," Zack said stiffly. "Nice flowers."

"West," Ian returned. He finally pivoted to acknowledge Zack, his smile losing some of its luster. "You'll have to forgive me; I didn't bring you any. It's a bit of an odd tradition of mine, but I only get flowers for the investigators who find the killers. You'll get yours one day. I hope..."

Carlee was worried the bad blood in the room was about to boil over, but it didn't seem bad enough to worry Alicia. She was too busy ogling Ian, pointing at him with one hand and covering the gesture with her other.

Holy shit, she mouthed exaggeratedly at Carlee. *Is* this *the guy?*

Carlee was seconds away from hauling herself out of bed to actually pinch her when Ian started laughing. Her heart dropped, and she whipped her head back to Officer Friendly and Agent Hollywood, expecting a fistfight.

"I hear you, Garnett," Zack said, chuckling. "Maybe next time." He walked over and clapped Ian on the shoulder.

Ian hunched at the contact but didn't launch any retort. At least they were keeping things civil in her hospital room, barbed comments aside.

Ian only shook his head and moved to place the flowers on Carlee's bedside table. Then, shockingly, he warmly squeezed her upper arm and gave her what she could only assume was his most encouraging smile. Damn it, she had to admit it was radiant.

"Two murder attempts in as many months is a bit much for a PI, don't you think?" he asked, cocking an eyebrow.

"And the flowers are a bit much for a work colleague, don't *you* think?" Carlee returned, but regretted it a little when Ian's buoyancy fell. "Though lilies are my favorite."

"I know," he said with a wink. Then, leaving her perplexed, he fluffed the flowers and turned his attention to Alicia.

As the two of them nattered about mundane niceties, Ian asking Alicia what she did for a living and Alicia delighting Ian with questions about life at the FBI, Carlee looked for Zack. She wanted to say *something*—something to clear the air, to cheer him up, to let him know it would be all right between them, to tell him not to pay any attention to Garnett's bullshit. But her good mood evaporated when she noticed Zack had disappeared from the room.

She craned her neck and saw him in the hall on his phone, pacing back and forth. Judging from how much his eyebrows pinched, it was a serious work matter.

At that moment, as if he had felt her gaze, Zack looked up with a grave expression written thickly across his face. Their eyes met, and he shook his head, mouthing, *"I have to go."*

A pit formed in her stomach as he took off down the hall and away from her.

"Zack, wait!" Carlee called, but it was too late.

It didn't matter, she supposed, if they spoke the words to each other or not.

The look he had given her told her all she needed to know.

It had something to do with the Eighth-Grade Killer.

Chapter Twenty-Nine

I tilted the mug up and up and up until the last dregs of morning coffee slid down my tongue. Usually, this was the worst sip, the bitterest, the part with little bits of bean along for the ride. Not today, though. It was all good today.

I folded my paper, placed it to the side, got up, and washed the mug in the sink. I took my time, like always, making sure it was spotless. No matter how excited I was, everything had to be done at its own pace.

A tingle of excitement shook my hand as I placed the mug on the drying rack. Today was a special day—so special that I had almost forgone my routine to get to the festivities. But rushing made for messy work and mistakes, and I reviled few things more than messiness.

I turned down the hall, past the linen closet with the toolbox. As I neared the door, I could feel my heart rate spike.

"You need to calm down," chided the imaginary doctor in my head, as if tough love would get me to listen.

"I can't," I whispered aloud with the faintest hint of a smile.

I turned the dead bolt, and it slid open with a satisfying thump. There was a weight to it, one I felt mirrored my intentions. I knew what I would do beyond this door, and the dead bolt symbolized my first real step toward that goal.

It also provided the tiniest thrill. Whenever I had a guest over, I always waited for them to ask, "Why is there a dead bolt on *this* door?" But no one ever had.

Why this door, a voice in my head asked as I turned the knob.

"Why, indeed," I answered back.

It was dark, nearly pitch black. I had long ago bricked up the small windows that lined the outside wall, and though I had made my way down these steps countless times, I took care not to trip. It wouldn't do me any good to break my neck and die in my basement. The thought of *that* being part of my legacy was enough to make me bide my time.

I reached the landing without incident, took the five steps to the center of the room, reached out my hand, and—there. The pull string.

I closed my eyes and took a deep breath, standing a little straighter as I tugged on the line and lit the room.

"Good," I said as I looked around and inspected my preparations. The single lightbulb barely lit the space, but that was the way I liked it. Perhaps it was a guilty pleasure, but moody lighting and stark cinderblock walls met the standards of what I thought was a good setting for a horror story. It was one of my few indulgences.

A draft flapped at one of the tarp's corners, and I went to the shelves to grab some duct tape and secure it. I couldn't have it moving out of place and ruining the video. I only got one chance at a cinematic masterpiece.

As I yanked the tape free from its roll, a muffled cry sounded from the adjoining room, and I had to pause for a moment to settle myself.

"You'll have to wait," I said as soothingly as possible. It didn't appear to help, but that wasn't my responsibility. Not yet.

Once the tarp was secure, I took the stool and placed it delicately in its center, underneath the light. I knew this would give me the best shadows.

Then I stepped up to the hardened case and began popping its latches. Each pop made me more and more excited, a Pavlovian reaction. Another pause, another deep breath, and I began to take the pieces out of the case.

First, the tripod, which I set at a precise distance from the stool—always the same. Then, the camera. The man who sold it to me thought I was a dedicated hobbyist. In a way, he wasn't wrong.

I couldn't help but imagine Carlee sitting on the stool, under my light, answering my questions. It was a thought that had been eating away at me for years. When the time came, I wondered if I'd film it. Of course, she would be the last victim, so there wouldn't be a real point.

A part of me wanted to be selfish, to keep that moment for myself. Another part of me knew the world needed to see the culmination of my work. Maybe then they'd understand it. Maybe then they'd learn the lesson I had been trying to teach them.

Yet another part knew it was wrong to deny Carlee the benefit of the whole experience. Her brother had gotten it. Most of her classmates had gotten it. Why shouldn't she?

I placed my camera on the tripod and adjusted the pitch to ensure a leveled shot. A quick check to make sure the battery wouldn't die on me halfway through, and I was ready. I approached the door where the muffled cries had now fallen silent.

"Please stay back and away from the door, sweetie," I said with more compassion than she deserved. "I don't think I need to remind you what happened last time?"

Slowly, I undid each lock before finally opening the door and stepping inside. It couldn't have been described as anything more than a concrete box. There was no light source in the room. The only things in it were the bucket, the dingy old futon she was now curled up on, and the plate, which still had a barely touched sandwich on it.

"Now, Adela, are you sure you don't want to eat this?" I asked calmly. There was no need to yell. Soon enough, it wouldn't make any difference if she ate or not. "Because I'll take it away if you don't want it."

Adela dipped her pretty round face and black curls behind her knees, trying her hardest to hide from me. I wanted to reach out and pull her face up, tell her she shouldn't hide like that. Tell her that she looked beautiful, like Carlee when she was her age.

"I'm not hungry," Adela stammered. She had left most of the meals I made for her untouched since I'd taken her, only a few days ago now.

"Then let's get up," I said, crossing the distance between us.

She flinched as I reached down to grab her arm. My grip was firm as I brought Adela to her feet, but she didn't need much directing. She stopped at the door, dug her heels in, and refused to move any farther.

I leaned down by her ear and whispered, "It's okay, I promise. I'm giving you permission this time."

Her timid steps signaled that she still didn't believe me. I couldn't blame her. The beating she'd received yesterday when she tried to dash from the room had been biblical, but much like a horse that needed to be tamed, she hadn't given me an ounce of trouble since.

I savored the sound of her feet sliding across the tarp. It sounded different each time, giving each experience a unique texture. Joel's footsteps had been heavier, slower, richer. Adela's were lighter, almost waifish. It matched her appearance to a tee.

Before I knew it, she was at the stool, and I helped her onto it. I leaned down to her eye level. Her gaze was vacant, barely registering me in front of her. I was a little annoyed, but I knew it wouldn't matter in the grand scheme of things, and the grand scheme was all that mattered.

"All right, Adela," I said, my cadence smooth. I pointed to the camera at the edge of the tarp. "I'm going to stand over there now and hold up some cue cards. I need you to read them for me."

She didn't nod, didn't acknowledge my words at all, but that was okay. I knew she would do what I asked without question, as they all did when I had complete power over them.

"Please read the words clearly—no mumbling, no stammering." I gripped her shoulder a smidgen tighter so she understood how important this was. "You have to say everything accurately. Word for word. Okay?"

No *yes* or *no*, no nod or shake in understanding, but I didn't need such things. I turned around and walked to the camera, working hard to control my breathing. My excitement was nearly beating out of my chest. I picked up the cards and turned toward Adela—still sitting quietly on the stool, waiting for my command. I had been depriving myself of this ever since I had killed Joel, and now, finally, I had a chance to bask in it again.

I thought back to the first time I had seen Adela—that day at the park near Carlee's place. She had been so mean to that poor little girl on the swings. It was apparent to me then that it was too late for Adela to learn how to be a decent human being and treat others correctly. So, when I found out she lived in Carlee's building, it seemed like fate.

My hand was unwavering as I turned the camera on and pointed it at Adela, her cue to begin a message that Carlee Knight wouldn't be able to ignore.

Chapter Thirty

Carlee sat at her desk, listening to a client's story. It had taken two weeks to begin seeing new clients after her latest ordeal. She would've started sooner, but Eleanor had put her foot down and forced her to take a break—however small.

Carlee winced at the thought and immediately regretted the wording, even if she hadn't said it aloud. Because there were no small cases, there were no small breaks. Everyone deserved justice, and every second she delayed robbed someone of their chance.

"I was *robbed* of the last six years of my life," the client said earnestly, making Carlee jump at the use of her own word. Candice Harkness, the sickly woman sitting across her desk, looked as if she hadn't eaten anything in years. As Carlee tuned back into Candice's story, she realized it wasn't far from the truth.

"I only came out of my coma a few weeks ago, and now, after hearing everything that's happened," Candice said, breath hitching, "I feel like none of it was an accident…"

Carlee couldn't lean across the desk and rub her arm, so instead, she said, "It's okay, Candice. Take your time."

"Time, huh? I've wasted enough time, don't you think?" Candice asked quietly. She sniffed and settled herself as much as she could.

Carlee got the impression she was a generally jittery person, or maybe jitters were a side effect of the coma. "I've mostly been in physical therapy learning how to live again."

"That must be so hard."

"I can't even begin to explain, but the hardest thing is all the thinking—a lot of thinking. And the more I think, the more I realize someone hit me with that car on purpose."

"I'm so sorry," Carlee said, "but I have to be blunt in my line of work. There are plenty of hit-and-run incidents throughout Chicago every day. Do you have any evidence that points to an attempt on your life rather than an unfortunate accident?"

"I have some leads," Candice said in a small flash of confidence. It flared away just as quickly, though, and she slumped into her chair. "I read in an interview of yours that you don't believe in coincidences, which is why I chose to come to you with this. Because believe me, Carlee, this can't be a coincidence. If you agree to work with me, you'll understand once I show you what I've found."

Coincidences burned in Carlee's ear. Candice spoke the truth: in her book, they had never existed. "Like what?"

"Like how my mom conveniently died right after my accident, and even now, six years later, *no one* can tell me how or why or anything about it."

"Okay, that does seem odd."

"Or like how my dad just straight-up disappeared without a trace, and I still can't locate him anywhere," Candice added, beginning to tear up. "Ever since I woke up it feels like my whole life has gone off the rails, and when it started to seem like someone had it out for me, I decided to ask for your help."

"That is definitely a lot of disasters in short order," Carlee said, nodding. "Do you have any idea who might have wanted to hurt you—or your family?"

"No! That's the worst part! I was a nobody. I still am!" Candice started rocking back and forth ever so slightly in her chair, and Carlee's heart ached just watching it. "But now, I *swear* people duck into doorways and behind fences."

"What people?"

"All the people!" Her fear twisted into rage. "Cars follow me around and I can't step out of my front door without getting this overwhelming feeling that someone is watching me."

"Are you in touch with anyone who knew you from back then?" Carlee hoped so, since she clearly needed a lot of support.

"I am, but I don't know who to trust anymore." Candice sighed, shaking her head. "I just need to get some answers, Carlee. I need to... to figure this out so I can live again."

There was a cough from the door, and Carlee had to work hard not to stare down the person responsible. These days, the bigger a case got, the less Eleanor wanted her to take it. At the end of the day, though, it was her firm, and she would do what she thought was right.

"Candice, I can't imagine what you've been going through since you woke up and realized that six years had passed," Carlee said, eyeing Eleanor in the doorway. Behind Candice's shoulder, Eleanor pointed at her watch to signify the allotted consultation time was up. "And I feel compelled to help you, but let me do some preliminary digging before I decide if I can take on your case."

"How long will it take?" Candice asked, her eyes widening. It was probably the first good news she'd had in an age, and she smiled for the first time since walking into Carlee's office.

"Not long. Just give me a few days," Carlee said, flashing Candice her warmest smile. "Eleanor, would you mind taking down Candice's details and seeing her to the door?"

"Of course," Eleanor said in a brisk, bright tone that meant she was displeased, then she asked Candice to follow her.

With a shaky thank you, Candice made her way out, her legs still undoubtedly frail from disuse. Carlee almost got up in a rush to help, but seeing Eleanor had it handled, she kept herself firmly planted in her chair.

The outer door opened and closed, signifying Eleanor had escorted Candice out, and a few seconds later, she came back into Carlee's office.

"You're not seriously thinking about taking the case, are you? The woman is insane!" Eleanor propped her back against the wall, not quite hovering but close enough to make Carlee nervous.

"If you're going to loom over me, you might as well take a seat, Eleanor," she said. "You don't have to pretend like you're not here. I'm not going to snap at you or anything."

"Because you know better than to snap at me," Eleanor said coyly. Her words were an odd mix of lightness and apprehension—they were both unsure if they should be mad at each other.

Carlee wanted to feel annoyed at Eleanor's overbearing behavior since her run-in with the Two-Faced Killer and insist she give her some space, but part of her had to admit she had a valid reason for hovering. It had been a hell of a couple of months.

And that was *without* accounting for the possible return of the Eighth-Grade Killer, which Carlee was still in the dark about.

If the phone call Zack took in the hospital had indeed been about the Eighth-Grade Killer case, he wasn't looping her in on any of the new details. They'd spoken several times in the past couple of weeks, and everything certainly seemed smoother between them since their fight and her near-death experience. But Carlee was beginning to feel he was withholding things from her now, treating her like a victim instead of a fellow investigator.

"You don't want me to take it?" Carlee asked, regarding Eleanor across the desk.

"You know I don't," Eleanor said evenly. "I want you to take the Strong case—a nice and easy infidelity bit—but you pawned her off on Bob Stevens."

"Bob Stevens is the best infidelity PI in the greater Chicago area," Carlee said, fighting hard to control a smirk. "Why wouldn't I refer her to Bob?"

"Because *you're* the best infidelity PI in the greater Chicago area," Eleanor said, her exasperation growing. "I don't know why you insist on taking these dangerous cases."

"Because I'm one of the *best* PIs in Chicago, regardless of the case," Carlee said definitively. There were few things in Carlee's life she was completely confident in—difficult conversations with people close to her decidedly not among them—but she was confident in her abilities as an investigator. "And I take big cases because I can do some good. There isn't much good to do with the Strong case beyond taking a picture of the husband's bald behind banging his secretary."

Eleanor arched a brow. "Maybe, but I bet Mr. Bald Behind won't end up drugging you," she insisted. "I bet he won't give you a scar on your neck, either. And I see you pawing at it when you think no one is looking."

"Look, Eleanor..." Carlee slumped her shoulders, tired of fighting. "I know you want me to be safe, and I promise you I will be. But I know my skills can make a difference in cases like Candice's. And if I think I can bring about some justice, I'm going to do that. I'm not saying I'll take it, but I am going to look into it, and I am sorry if it worries you."

Eleanor sat primly in the chair across from Carlee, quiet for a moment. Then, finally, she nodded begrudgingly. "I guess if I can't stop you, I've got to file Candice Harkness's form." She stood up and walked out, not waiting around for another argument.

Carlee sighed and rubbed her hand down her face. She didn't know how much longer she would be able to stand such an icy office.

She rolled her shoulder, about to get to work on a deep dive into Candice's accident, when a smear of red across the street caught her eye. It hadn't been there when Candice Harkness walked out a few moments ago, and Carlee's chin snapped toward her window to take a closer look.

A banner had been unfurled over the access bridge of the medical complex directly across from her, a new advertising campaign beaming directly into the Knight offices. As if it was especially for her.

Her heart raced as she walked up to her window and peered out. Oversized capital letters had been written across the banner, big enough that she could read them, and some of the font color dripped off the canvas and onto the glass below it.

Her blood ran cold.

A sense of calm sluiced over Carlee as she read each word, but not the calm someone felt when they were safe. It was the type of calm that came with knowing they couldn't avoid the tsunami hurtling toward them. When they knew beyond a shadow of a doubt they were going to be pulled under, and they accepted it.

I'M SICK OF HIDING, CARLEE, the red words said.
AREN'T YOU?

The End

• • • ● ● • ● ● • • •

All of the Harborside Secrets Series books can be found on Amazon.

What's Next

<u>Book 4 - *The Faceless Killer*</u>

Serial murderers don't hesitate—but neither does Carlee Knight. With one click, you can join her fevered hunt for the Faceless Killer in book four of Katy Pierce's Harborside Secrets!

The Faceless Killer - Book 4 of my Harborside Secrets series - is available on Amazon.

Scan the QR code below to grab your copy now!

Free Prequel - *The Unexpected Killer*

Do you want to know what stands behind Carlee's constant lack of trust in people? It's the only way to understand why she's struggling to overcome it.

If you're brave enough, you can travel back in time to the younger version of Carlee, and let her show you.

***The Unexpected Killer*- the Prequel of my Harborside Secrets series - is free for download!**

Scan the QR code below to grab your copy now!

THE TWO-FACED KILLER

A Note From The Author

Mind if we chat?

I truly hope this adventure with Carlee Knight thrilled you, surprised you, and tantalized you with a few brain-busting clues! Now that you've come to the end of the book and have had some time to breathe, I wanted to let you know how grateful I am to have you as a reader. This is a very special moment in my life. I've worked on improving my craft and have sent my new work off into the big, bad world. It's exhilarating, but it's also terrifying. Words cannot express what a relief it is to know I don't have to do this alone. Your support means the world to me, and I would never have made it this far without you. THANK YOU for coming with me on Carlee's adventures. It's my adventure, too—and it's also yours. Your opinions, ideas, responses, and reactions are what fuel my courage to keep writing. They are priceless to me, and each comment makes me a stronger, braver writer. If you have the time to leave me a review on Amazon, please know I always love to hear your thoughts. I read every review I receive-SERIOUSLY. In fact, I think I might have a problem. ;)

To make it a little easier, you can scan the QR code below to review!

Thank you again for everything. I'm so glad to be here, following Carlee with you.

Katy

Acknowledgments

I'd like to end this book by thanking the person who helps me do what I do, my dear and wonderful husband.

You are the love of my life and my soul mate. You stood beside me with each and every step of my challenging life journey and I think you deserve a medal for that!

I love you,
Katy.

About the Author

Katy Pierce is a born and raised New Yorker. Most of the time, she is a passionate, outspoken, cynical woman, but all that fades away when she comes home to her husband and two kids at the end of a long day, where she willingly turns into a cliché, soaking in every second of motherhood life has to offer.

For Katy, creative block is considered a hoax, since from the second she wakes up, new ideas keep coming to her, characters she never met before are driving her crazy and in a perfect world, she'd be writing books 24/7.

She enjoys the simple things like making her husband proud, making her children laugh, and making her readers gasp for air as they flip through the pages of her fictional creations. She's addicted to social media, has a terrible fear of spiders, and would rather speak her mind and be hated for it than keep quiet and fake being "normal". Come to think of it, she hates the word "normal".

When Katy writes, it's as if the whole world comes to a complete halt. In her mind, the stories, the emotions, and life-threatening situations are real. She can see it all and she simply writes what she sees.

With every new book of hers that gets published, Katy feels she can breathe just a little bit deeper than before, which is why she vows to keep at it for as long as humanly possible.

<u>Scan the following QR code to follow Katy on social media:</u>

Made in the USA
Columbia, SC
08 November 2023